Please renew/return this item by the last date shown.

So that your telephone call is charged at local rate,
please call the numbers as set out below:

	From Area codes 01923 or 0208:	From the rest of Herts:
Renewals:	01923 471373	01438 737373
Enquiries:	01923 471333	01438 737333
Minicom:	01923 471599	01438 737599

L32b

D1436083

Ghosts Over Britain

GHOSTS OVER BRITAIN

Peter Moss

Illustrated by Angela Lewer

Elm Tree Books · London

First published in Great Britain in 1977 by Elm Tree Books/Hamish Hamilton Ltd.
90 Great Russell Street, London WC1B 3PT in association with Book Club
Associates

Photographs by Rathbone Studios
Designed by Harold Bartram

Printed in Great Britain by
GPS Print Ltd. London

Contents

Introduction

Introduction

More than two years ago on a summer's evening, having just finished one of my wife's splendid dinners, my guests and I were talking lazily over our brandy when the question of ghosts arose. There seems to be a universal fascination with the unknown, and my friends were as intrigued as I was by the prospect of a modern ghost. Do people still see ghosts—*new* ghosts, that is—and if they do, where do they see them and what are they like? Not realising just where it would lead us, my publisher, who was present at the time, and I decided to start a ghost hunt.

I began by advertising in local newspapers—asking people with recent experiences of the supernatural to get in touch with me—and the response was tremendous. This led to more adverts all over Britain—and *hundreds* of letters. Not only did this massive response reveal the depth of feeling on the subject, but also gave the lie to the stereotype of the person who had paranormal experiences as a disturbed, frustrated, ill-educated old spinster. In fact, the people who responded cut across all the divisions of age, class, education, occupation and geography, and if women do outnumber men by about two to one, this may have more to do with the fact that in most families it is the wife who is the letter writer.

What rapidly emerged from the flood of letters and telephone calls was that the supernatural is experienced more widely than ever before, but that the 'ghosts' are not always of a traditional form. The classical phantom, that filmy apparition, usually headless, tends to be of noble birth, and disdains to appear anywhere but in the castles and mansions of the great. The contemporary haunt, on the other hand, has accepted an age of democracy and equality, and modern psychic experiences tend to occur in more mundane circumstances—new flats, old tenements, council houses, suburban semis, the public lavatory of a motorway service station and stark secondary schools. The contemporary ghost is bolder too, often spurning the night: more than a third of the cases reported took place in broad daylight.

The compiler of an anthology of psychic phenomena must always be on the alert for the deliberately invented story, or the account which has been elaborated, perhaps quite unconsciously, from a real or imagined incident. One factor which has been consistent throughout the correspondence with those who have offered to share their experiences is the utter sincerity of their beliefs. However, sincerity is obviously not enough to confirm a report of the supernatural, and the problems of selection have been difficult. Finally, I chose the ones which had corroborative evidence of some kind. Sometimes this has been the presence of more than one witness; sometimes the appearance of the phenomenon on more than one occasion to the same witness; and sometimes from purely factual evidence from outside sources which support the report.

Often the experiences submitted were trivial and apparently meaningless, without antecedent or aftermath, and frequently the experiences were bizarre. But their strangeness and triviality often served only to add to their authenticity: why make up something which appears meaningless? And with the innate human dislike of the irrational, why describe such bizarre incidents as an eye peering through a hole in a floorboard or gouts of blood falling from a perfect and unmarked kitchen ceiling?

Fascination with the supernatural is a powerful force in man, who tries endlessly to rationalise these occurrences. The supernatural, which once could find a home in every stone and tree and stream, has been forced to retreat deeper and deeper into the remote parts of the earth, to the depths of the ocean and to space itself. Even the mind, the last bastion of the unknown, has been besieged by the psychologist, anxious to impose reason and order there. Yet belief in the supernatural was never stronger, never more avidly sought after, than it is in our society today. The fact that today's ghost may be seen in a council house or a school, rather than in an ancient, ancestral home; or may look like you or me, rather than a vague, shadowy apparition—doesn't make it any more explicable, only more up-to-date.

So I offer you some 60 experiences of the supernatural—all but a few of which are totally original and never reported before. These are genuine and sincere reports, as told to me by the people who experienced them. In one or two cases names in the accounts have been changed at the request of the contributor. However, the names of the contributors themselves are genuine and given in all cases except where anonymity was requested.

P.M.

Shadows of Violence

The Suicide Room

In May 1971 Rosaleen Morrison, an Edinburgh barrister, was staying with her sister in London, and had been asked as a matter of domestic expediency if she could sleep somewhere else for one night. A nearby hotel was the obvious answer but Rosaleen recalled that an old friend, Winston Hemmingsley, had just taken a flat in Red Lion Square for a couple of months, and had previously pressed her to stay there if ever she was at a loose end in London. The tenants of the flat, a Dr Rosemary W. and a medical student who shared it with her, were to be away, separately, for about eight weeks, and felt that letting it to a slight acquaintance was preferable to leaving it as an open temptation to vandals and squatters.

Rosaleen telephoned on the Friday morning to ask Winston if it would be convenient for her to stay with him that evening, but the response she received was not encouraging. Winston seemed pre-occupied and reluctant despite the cordiality of his previous invitation, but eventually, and unconvincingly, said that she would be welcome. She could not guess at the reason for the change in attitude: Rosaleen was aware that he had for some time shared the flat with a girl, Heather —on a strictly platonic basis—so that embarrassment, prudery or fear of criticism were not the reasons. She was a little dismayed when she did arrive at Red Lion Square about 5pm that evening. The flat, obviously designed for a single person, with one small bedroom, a sitting room, bathroom and kitchen, was stretched to accommodate two: three seemed impossible with decency. But the physical problems were heightened by the psychological ones: Winston and Heather seemed extremely uneasy for no apparent reason, and the earlier pre-occupation had developed into an inhibiting tension.

Winston explained that Heather did not like the bedroom (which was normally occupied by the medical student), and was sleeping on the divan in the sitting room (normally used by Dr W.), while he had a sleeping bag on the floor. He urged Rosaleen that it would be 'cosier' if she joined them in the sitting room, but this bizarre *ménage a trois*, even if divorced from all sexual implications, conflicted with her conceptions of dignity and decorum, and there was a perfectly good bed in the next room. With some emphasis she insisted on using the bedroom, if it was definitely not occupied.

The instant she entered it, however, she could appreciate Heather's disquiet: it could only be described as stark, and with carpet, walls and ceiling all in dark blue it gave an impression of claustrophobic gloom. There were no curtains at the window apart from some almost-transparent net, and the only furniture was a small desk and a single bed, from which all of the bedding apart from a quilt and a sheet had been removed. Several whimsy pictures of flower fairies hung crookedly from the walls, and on the mantelpiece were several photographs, among them one of an attractive girl with short hair, sitting in the front seat of an open car looking at two large dogs in the back. All of this, and an intangible unpleasantness, made Rosaleen uneasy.

Turning to Winston who had followed her into the room she asked casually if the photograph was of Dr Rosemary, but he said that he thought it was of her flatmate, the medical student. He apologised for the lack of blankets, saying that they were all at the laundry, and on that count again urged her to sleep in the lounge where it would be warmer. When Rosaleen said that she would be content with the quilt and her overcoat for the one night, he conceded victory. Their evening meal was taken at a restaurant, and later back at the flat they talked until the early hours of the morning, when Winston made a last effort to get Rosaleen to join himself and Heather in the sitting room. Now slightly suspicious of his intentions, she rejected the suggestion more firmly than ever, and went to bed.

Always uncomfortable in an unfamiliar room, she found difficulty in getting to sleep: the unrelenting light streamed in through the window; the unaccustomed and inadequate bedding left her chilly, and she was unaccountably disturbed by the whole of the evening's events. Nevertheless, after some time she did fall into a doze, only to be roused soon afterwards by the sensation of someone's hair brushing her face. As she opened her eyes she was conscious first of that slight change in the quality of the light that suggests the imminence of dawn, and then of a person bending over her. Her immediate reaction in the confusion of waking was that Winston was attempting to seduce her, but his innocence was established at once when she recognised the young woman of the photograph on the mantelpiece, who now had long hair. Rosaleen knew at once that there must have been some mistake with the dates, and that the medical student, returning late from a party, had come home to bed.

'Who are you?' Rosaleen demanded instinctively, using speech more to cover her embarrassment than to seek information and feeling at the same time a wave of annoyance at Winston for being so stupid as to make such a mistake. The girl reached out to grasp the top of the bedclothes to pull them back, and replied, 'I'm Hillary, and what are you doing in my bed?' The whole encounter was completely rational,

Rosaleen Morrison at the scene of the suicide room.

even if acutely uncomfortable, and Rosaleen felt that she must at least offer some vindication of herself. 'Winston and Heather said I could stay here,' she said, 'it's only for one night. I'm very sorry, I did not mean to take your bed.' 'Oh—you mean there are others here too?' asked Hillary, then sadly, wearily she added, 'Oh dear . . .', and straightening up she moved towards the door, apparently to discuss the matter with Winston.

Despite her anger towards Winston, her personal embarrassment, and her pity for the girl, all of which seethed in turmoil inside her, Rosaleen, seduced by sleep, closed her eyes and was conscious of no more of the argument until she was wakened at 11am the following morning by Winston who said that she was wanted on the phone. As she passed through the sitting room she complained that the night had been bad enough without having been forced into the position of stealing someone's bed. She made some brief but acrimonious comments about not being told that Hillary might return, and how guilty she felt.

Coming back from the telephone she was aware that there had been a change in the atmosphere: the tension had now turned into something more frightening. She was asked to repeat what she had said: Winston's face was white and frozen, and without a word he crossed to the phone to speak to Dr W. Rosaleen heard Hillary's name mentioned, but the rest of the conversation was a series of deliberately non-committal comments. Even whiter than before he turned to Rosaleen and asked flatly, 'How did you know Rosemary's flatmate's name was Hillary? I have never mentioned it to you. And whoever came into the flat last night couldn't have been Hillary—she is in hospital, not expected to live. She tried to commit suicide in her bedroom a few days ago by slashing her wrists, and was taken away the day before we moved in. When we arrived later the place was indescribable—there was blood from the bathroom to the bedroom, splashes on the carpet, curtains and walls, and the bedding was soaked. We spent the day cleaning up, scrubbing down, and taking everything we could move to the laundry —that's why we were so strange when you rang. We were furious about Rosemary, and I said some pretty harsh things when we got to the salon—until one of my assistants told me he had just heard from Rosemary what had happened.'

Despite the intense strain on their faces, Rosaleen could not help believing the whole thing was a hideous, obscene joke, until Winston took her back into the bedroom and showed her in the light of day what had escaped her in the dimness of the evening before. There were still spots of blood on the carpet and walls, and terrifyingly, on the desk a small wooden-handled dagger with the rust of blood on its blade. When Winston pulled back the quilt to show that there was a great dark stain on it which had been hidden by the sheet, Rosaleen's deep feeling of pity turned first to intense revulsion, and then of black anger towards Winston for having allowed her to sleep under it. Then, when he pulled back the curtain across the alcove at the head of the bed to reveal Hillary's yellow broderie anglaise evening dress saturated about its hem with browning blood, she was again swamped by immense pity at the sheer pointlessness of it all.

It was some months later amid the sanity of her work in Edinburgh that the last scene of the Kafkaesque nightmare was played out. Visiting Rosaleen, Winston confessed that he had been lying that morning when he reported that Hillary was unconscious in hospital: she had indeed died during that night, but he feared for all three if he had made this known.

Rosaleen Morrison, Edinburgh

While of Unsound Mind

In the world of hauntings, the apparitions of suicides figure prominently, which is not surprising, for of all human actions the taking of one's own life must be the most desperate. That some fragment of this anguish should linger, consciously or unconsciously, is very understandable.

In 1955 Alan Bogue, a 19-year-old apprentice painter, had been sent with a skilled craftsman, Bill Oliver, to an early Victorian house in Garscube Terrace, Edinburgh, to redecorate a small, unoccupied but fully-furnished flat on the top floor. On the first day Bill had gone down to the basement to make tea for the mid-morning break, leaving Alan in the bathroom cleaning up splashes on the floor. On hands and knees Alan backed towards the doorway, automatically rubbing with his turpentine-soaked rag, when he heard the sound of bare feet walking lightly along the passage from the bed-sitting-room; there was the slight 'stickiness' as each foot was lifted from the linoleum. Although he had thought he was alone on the fourth floor, there was no reason why someone else should not be there, and he took little notice.

Then, in the next instant three events happened almost simultaneously: he reached the architrave of the doorway as he worked back; the footsteps came up level with him, and he was immediately hit by what he can only describe as a powerful electric shock. There was a blinding, stunning flash of brilliant light, which was felt almost as something tangible inside his brain rather than seen through his eyes, and his body was momentarily paralysed by a violent spasm. Alan staggered to his feet, dazed, and lurched towards the bed-sitting-room to sit down to recover. As he approached the door, the handle moved downwards and the door itself opened: in the confusion of the moment the facts registered in his mind, but their significance did not. He stumbled inside—he is not sure now whether he closed the door himself or not—and sat on the bed for a few moments. When he had recovered, the strange behaviour of the door puzzled him, and he looked round to find out why it had opened in front of him. As the window was closed there could have been no gust of wind, so that he assumed there must be some quirk in the carpentry that caused his weight on the floorboards to let slip the catch.

With that issue settled logically, if not very convincingly, he stood up to return to the job, wondering about the more important incident. There were certainly no electrical wires or equipment anywhere near where he had been working, so that a normal shock from the mains was ruled out, and it was with some trepidation that he approached the bathroom again, and bent down. Instantly there came the same flash and tingling, though on this second occasion not as powerful as the first.

As he stood up the intense feelings of amazement and alarm were suddenly overwhelmed by a deep sensation of inexplicable grief that came from nowhere, and brought him to the verge of tears.

It was at this moment that Bill Oliver returned from the basement with the tray of tea, and seeing Alan obviously in a strange state of shock and depression, he made some light-hearted comment. When Alan replied that he thought the bathroom was haunted, the reaction was electrifying: Bill's face suddenly drained of all colour, he dropped the tray, which fell down the stair well to crash to the hall four storeys below, and then, with a rising flush of anger, he flew at Alan's throat with hands outstretched like a man demented.

After a brief struggle the insane mood passed: Bill apologised and said that for the moment the shock of what Alan had said had made him lose control of himself. He explained that while he had been preparing the tea the lady who owned the house had told him that the flat they were working on was being redecorated because three weeks earlier the tenant, a young history teacher, Anne D., had committed suicide by hanging herself from the bathroom door by her dressing gown cord—a desperate act precipitated, Alan later learned, by a letter from her fiance breaking off their engagement.

Neither man saw anything abnormal for the rest of the time they were working in the house, but Alan says that for the whole while he was unable to rid himself of the profound sadness.

Alan J Bogue, Edinburgh

Facsimile of Murder

The vast majority of reports of the supernatural concern visible and audible phenomena—apparitions, lights, footsteps, rappings and occasionally speech: much more rare are the cases in which the senses of smell and touch are involved, unless, that is, the frequently-reported fall in temperature associated with psychic events can be considered a tactile sensation. But there are experiences beyond these which should be considered under the heading of 'hauntings' even if it means a reappraisal of our traditional interpretation of the term.

The ordeal that Geoffrey Wright of Colchester underwent in November 1975 must, by its context, be classed as a crisis haunting, but the strange way in which the events worked themselves out places it in a category all of its own. At some unknown time during the night of Thursday, 27 November, 1975, Geoffrey's widowed mother, Mrs Edith Wright, was savagely murdered by her stepson, Kevin Wright in

Geoffrey Wright at home.

her flat at Lilac Court, Colchester. Kevin Wright was arrested soon after the crime became known, and in March 1976 was found guilty of manslaughter on the grounds of diminished responsibility, and was sentenced to be detained for life in a criminal mental institution. The act was obviously that of a psychopath as Mrs Wright had been savagely assaulted, stabbed and finally drowned in her bath. The body was pushed under her bed and left: it was not until Sunday, two days later, that neighbours became suspicious about her absence, and later in the day the police broke in to discover the body.

At the time her son Geoffrey, aged 24, was in St Bartholomew's Hospital in London for observation: he was not ill, but his doctor, baffled by certain symptoms, felt that he should be given some tests in a specialist hospital. Although Geoffrey lived only a few hundred yards away from his mother's flat in the huge Greenstead estate, he saw her only infrequently. His childhood had not been a happy one, and the break-up of the family had introduced strains that left a wide gap between the two, bridged only on formal occasions. Thursday, 27 November was much as most days in hospital were for Geoffrey; the waking hours were punctuated by meals, but otherwise the main problem was disposing of time—in and out of bed, walking round the ward, visiting the day room, watching television, reading and talking. The night staff, supper and lights-out came round in routine sequence until sleep ended another day.

Normally a sound, all-night sleeper, Geoffrey was drowsily surprised to come to consciousness finding himself being helped into bed in the early hours of Friday morning while the rest of the ward was wrapped in sleep. He had been found, the nurses told him, asleep under a bed at the far end of the room: no-one had seen or heard him go so that it was impossible to say how long he had been lying there. The whole of the right side of his face was extremely tender, but it was not until the morning that it was found to be badly bruised, presumably the result of falling from his bed. But the doctor who examined him was puzzled because it seemed most improbable that anyone who had fallen with sufficient force to cause such damage would have remained asleep, or would have crawled the length of the ward without being aware of it.

The day staff probably attributed Geoffrey's lack of appetite at breakfast time on Friday to his disturbed night, but when at lunch, tea and supper he still complained of feeling full almost to choking, they probably suspected some other, clinical cause. This sense of repletion lasted all day Saturday and most of Sunday. When on Sunday afternoon his wife visited him and told him that his mother could not be found, the news created little impression as there was no suggestion yet that anything might be seriously wrong. It was not until just before midnight that he heard of the tragedy, and only then because it was known that in the morning the story would be in the national newspapers which Geoffrey would certainly read. Immediately his appetite returned to normal.

The final incident in this bizarre tale was not told until July 1976 when Mrs Wright's affairs were being finally settled. Geoffrey was going through papers relating to his mother's death when he came across a report on the post mortem examination of the body. In it the pathologist had stated that the corpse showed extensive bruising down the right side of the face.

Geoffrey Wright, Colchester

Lingering Death

Another account which reflects the way in which intolerable mental and physical anguish can survive in some psychic form comes from Bayswater, the very heart of the small-flat, bed-sitter territory—an area where perhaps loneliness and unhappiness are more concentrated than anywhere else in the city.

Number 6 Lonsdale Road, W.11, a small, Edwardian house now demolished was in the 1920s divided into three small furnished flats and a basement. For about five years the ground floor was occupied by a Mrs L Probert and her daughter Phaïs who was nineteen at the time of the incident. In October 1927 the two women had gone to bed when Phaïs became aware of a creaking sound in the room from the direction of the window. She sat up in bed, and to her surprise saw a heavy wickerwork rocking chair moving steadily to and fro as if someone had just got up from it. Knowing that this was impossible, she glanced instinctively to the window to see if it was open, knowing all the time that this was merely a flimsy and useless barricade against a growing fear because the chair was too heavy to be moved by anything less than a gale.

But the window, as she knew full well, was not responsible, and in any case, the night was still. Yet when Phaïs rather reluctantly got out of bed to investigate further, she was immediately conscious of faint waves of air pulsing across the room in the semi-darkness, as if the draught was in some strange way blowing in slow, rhythmic puffs. At the same time she was conscious as each light air reached her of a foetid smell.

Now quite alarmed, she went towards the chair, whose motion was gradually diminishing, and as she neared the window she felt the faint beating of the draught a little more strongly as if something was flapping back and forwards, and the stench of corruption grew almost intolerable. In the half light she searched for something organic a stray cat might have brought in through the low window during the day, but could find nothing. Puzzled, she went back to bed, and in the morning the offensive smell and the ebb and flow of the air had vanished. The whole affair was dismissed—until two years later at almost the same date, when the mysterious phenomena were repeated.

A few days later Phaïs was in the local butcher's shop a little further along the street, and half-jokingly suggested that the butcher should keep his old, high bones more securely shut up as cats seemed to be dragging them into nearby houses, causing a most unpleasant smell. After hearing an account of the happenings in the Proberts' flat, the butcher paused, glanced up and said seriously, 'That house is supposed to be haunted.' Phaïs, still half-humorously, replied that they might have been told before, as she and her mother might not have taken it

17

had they been aware of its reputation. But there was no levity in the butcher's voice as he answered: 'Just over a year before you moved in a middle-aged man living alone in your flat committed suicide by hanging himself from a hook near the window of the bedroom. His body hung there for a fortnight before anyone missed him, and they say that the stench when the police broke in was terrible. A couple took it over soon after, but they left suddenly and without giving any reason after a short stay . . .'

Phaïs Probert, Brighton

The Dying Cavalier

The English civil war stirred up savage emotions and left a legacy of bitterness seemingly out of proportion to the casualty lists and material damage caused, regrettable though both of these were. This may be because it completely divided the nation, and even more because it split devoted families into opposed factions, sometimes called on to slaughter one another. Support for one side or the other was, however, largely determined by region, by class and by occupation: sympathy for the king was generally strongest in rural areas, while Parliament had a considerable following in many towns. The pattern was, of course, subject to other factors, and in West Sussex the picture was very confused: parliamentary troops marched and countermarched through the countryside, while the king's men, largely through apathy, held, if feebly, towns such as Horsham and Chichester. As Cromwellian forces began to gain the upper hand, the busy little port of Siddlesham on Pagham Harbour, five miles south of Chichester, became an important staging post for royalists escaping with news or their services to other parts of the country. The inn which stood on the site of the present Crab and Lobster became the nerve centre for this underground operation.

When Chichester, the last main royalist stronghold in the area fell after a short siege there was a flurry of activity in Siddlesham as isolated cavaliers broke through the enemy lines and ran for safety. Among them was Sir Robert Earnley, his two nephews and two unknown gentlemen who, waiting at the tavern for a boat, were surprised by a patrol of parliamentary troopers. In a running fight outside all five were shot down in the roadway, though it is thought they were taken inside the inn to expire in relative comfort. For many years there were vague reports of a tall figure with a cloak and tight-fitting clothes seen flitting

The Crab and Lobster Inn.

both inside and outside the inn, but it was suggested that as seafaring custom disappeared with the silting up of the harbour in the late nineteenth century, a little publicity was a matter of commercial expediency. When Captain Peter Robinson became landlord in 1965 however, the haunting became much more credible, and tourists flocking to the Pagham Harbour nature reserve cut the ground from under the cynics' feet.

From the very first Captain Robinson's siamese cat behaved very oddly, particularly in the saloon where it always skirted parts of the floor and from time to time leapt in great terror to a chair as if trying to avoid something that it alone could see. One room upstairs had to be abandoned because of an inexplicably unpleasant atmosphere; heavy footsteps prowled downstairs at night, but when the landlord went to investigate armed with a shotgun, everything was quiet, bolted and barred.

Confirmation that these were due to supernatural causes came in a remarkable way in the summer of 1969 when a man and his wife, like hundreds of others in the season called for a meal at the Crab and Lobster. As they followed the landlord behind the bar to the dining room, the lady suddenly gasped loudly, and stood transfixed, gazing out into the saloon. After a moment she gathered herself together, and without further comment went in to dinner. After the meal she asked Captain Robinson if he would join them for coffee, and immediately inquired whether the place was haunted. When asked why she should think it was, she replied that as she had looked out from behind the bar she had seen a man in cavalier costume lying on the floor of the saloon, obviously close to death, but still struggling feebly to staunch with an inadequate handkerchief the blood which spurted from a gaping bullet hole in his chest.

It was only after the visitors had gone that Captain Robinson realised he had not asked who they were: the name 'Windsor' on the meal ticket did not mean anything to him, but it did to the wife of a senior police officer who had listened to the conversation. 'Of course,' she said, 'I should have recognised that face—it was Nora Windsor, the well-known medium.' Captain Peter Robinson claims that he is completely insensitive to and sceptical of the supernatural, but he may have powers that he does not fully realise. His mother, he told me, was a deeply religious woman who throughout her life kept a diary of daily domestic trivia. For most of the war Captain Robinson was a prisoner in

The bar where the 'Cavalier' died.

Japanese hands, and after his release in 1945 his mother was going through her diary to bring him up to date on family affairs of the lost years. He noted two entries, separated by about twelve months, which read: 'Woke 2.30am and prayed for Peter.' Though he never told his mother, those days were the two on which he had been tortured in a punishment cell in the prison camp.

Captain Peter Robinson, Crab and Lobster Inn, Siddlesham, Sussex

Second Hand Ghost

Many local newspapers, particularly in the sprawling, anonymous cities, seem preoccupied with the more sordid aspects of life—crime, violence, sex, drunkenness and squalor. Those circulating in west London, which is a particularly fertile field for reporting of this genre, greeted the new year 1966 with a story which embraced half a dozen facets of nastiness all in one scoop. Minor mayhem went inside as front pages were cleared for court details of the murder of an elderly widow whose naked and battered body had been found in the basement of a disused Methodist chapel a month earlier.

On Saturday, 4 December, 1965, the woman, it seems, had celebrated the feast of St Nicholas a little prematurely and perhaps over-indulgently in a number of public houses in the district. She was seen leaving the Old Oak Inn in North End Road about 10.15pm with a 30-year-old labourer who, inappropriately enough, lived and worked at a nearby Salvation Army hostel. Both were said by a witness who was close behind them, to be under the influence of drink, but not so much that their intentions were not clear in both of their minds.

When they arrived at the old chapel, which stood at the junction of North End Road with Chesson Road, the pair were seen to vanish into the basement, where the woman's body was discovered early the next day. The labourer was arrested almost immediately, making a lame and rather half-hearted attempt to explain away his blood-stained clothes and grazes by inventing a brawl with an unknown Scotsman. In a statement, however, he admitted that he and the woman had gone to the cellar to have sexual intercourse, but in an angry quarrel which had broken out over the fee for the lady's services, he must have lost his temper and killed her, though he remembered nothing. He was committed to the Old Bailey where he was found guilty, and with the appearance of an even more horrible homicide in the area, the events of the night passed from the minds of those not personally involved. The old chapel found a new, if short-lived lease on life as Second Hand City,

a market for used furniture and household bric-a-brac.

Frank Hastings, who was in charge of the antique section, was the first to believe that a shadowy shape in the main hall might be something more than random dust: when an identical form had appeared in the same place he realised that it must be a phantom, though at the time he was not aware of the tragedy of six years earlier. There did not appear to be a discernible face, though the figure wore a long dress, and there was some indication of a hood. If it was the ghost of the murdered woman, it did not give the feeling of remorse or regret —the whole atmosphere was one of happiness, delighting in Victorian surroundings.

The figure would often glide down the stairs to the basement where there was a fireplace and two nineteenth-century armchairs for the benefit of staff when business was quiet, and it was this area which seemed to be the favourite haunt of the ghost. It invariably disappeared near the fireplace, but could be seen sitting by the fire, long after the armchairs had gone. The night watchman and an upholsterer working late both reported independently the presence in exactly the same form and places as Mr Hastings had done.

But the ghost was capable of much more than mere appearance and disappearance: on one occasion Mr Hastings left a cup of tea in the basement restroom to serve a customer, and returned to find it half empty, though no one else had been near. On another occasion an employee passing the building at 3am saw the whole place ablaze with lights, though he knew the electricity had been switched off at the main before he left.

The old chapel was demolished in the 1970s but one wonders whether the elderly lady, born in its Victorian heyday, does not still linger near. An old lady with enough gusto for life at 65 to stick out to the end, undefeated for what she thought she was worth, should have enough spirit in another world to be a pretty persistent phantom.

Collated from diverse sources

'It could be seen sitting by the fire in a Victorian armchair.'

Supernatural Warnings

The Warning Ghost of Arrochar

The summer of 1946 was a bad one for eight-year-old Ian Irwin: in turn he had gone down with mumps and scarlet fever—diseases which even in the early antibiotic era were still claiming many deaths a year. In September he was taken by his mother and her parents to convalesce at an old house in Arrochar owned by a Mr Colquhoun, and here the delights of legitimately missing school and being raised to the dignity of adulthood by having a hotel room of his own, more than compensated for any discomforts he had suffered.

On the fourth night of his stay, Ian, accompanied by the Colquhoun dog, was dawdling along the top corridor towards what seemed to him an unjustifiably early bed when he became aware that one of the guests was following him. He heard no actual footsteps but was conscious, as people often are, that someone was behind him, and he turned with no more than mere curiosity to see who it was. The passage was completely empty, but as he looked along it slightly puzzled, the dog, with somewhat delayed reaction stopped its capering to stare with bristling hair and bared teeth towards the stair head. Assuming he had been mistaken, and not being old or experienced enough to realise that the dog's behaviour was suspicious, Ian went on and was immediately conscious of the presence again. Almost at once, however, he knew by some strange sense that it was no longer in the corridor but had entered a room whose door he had just passed. The dog began its gambolling again, and as Ian reached his own room it scampered back down the stairs.

Ian says that he remembers quite clearly the emotions that swept through him when he realised that he might have been in contact with the supernatural—excitement mixed with pride, fear and disbelief—but he was not sufficiently disturbed to go back down to his family or even to leave the light burning in his bedroom. Awake early the following morning, he went down to the hall where the proprietor was tidying up. The boy's calculatedly casual question, 'Is this house haunted?', brought a response which seemed out of all proportion to its importance. Extremely agitated Mr Colquhoun asked why the boy should say such a thing and where had he been sleeping. The mutual embarrassment was fortunately relieved a few moments later by the arrival of Ian's grandfather, who was somewhat surprised at having his morning greeting to the proprietor answered by the peremptory order to look to his grandson, who seemed to have had a shock. Ian was shrewd enough to realise at the time who had had the shock, but it was not until years later that he learned the explanation his grandfather had been given later that morning.

Towards the end of the eighteenth century, Colquhoun said, when the highlands were beginning to settle down after the savage repression of the 1745 rebellion, and the harshest of the restrictions imposed by the English were being eased, an earlier member of the family had set out from that house to walk to the clan gathering at Luss, some 9 miles away. A few miles along the way he realised that he had forgotten something and turned back, no doubt irritated that his own forgetfulness was costing him an hour or two's conviviality.

But annoyance turned to blind red fury as he entered his home and found his wife apparently in a compromising situation with a neighbour. In uncontrollable rage Colquhoun stabbed first his wife who, mortally injured, dragged herself along the upper passageway into one of the bedrooms, and then the neighbour. The whirlwind double slaughter took only seconds, and then the icy reaction set in as the dying friend gasped out the innocent purpose of his visit. A groom who had been in the house the whole time confirmed that no impropriety had taken place, and that the gesture had been one of genuine and kindly help.

In agonies of remorse Colquhoun wandered through the house until the following day when, just twenty-four hours after the death of his wife, he hanged himself. From then onwards, it was believed in the family that the dead woman made her presence felt to someone— though she seems never to have materialised—shortly before a death of a close member. In 1946 the apprehension seems to have been justified: the following day the proprietor's brother was killed in a road accident.

N I Irwin, Seaford, Sussex

Footsteps for Life

It is perhaps comforting to mortals to feel that some part of the spiritual world is conscious enough of them to intervene from time to time to warn or to prevent a tragedy. But the supernatural seems to use such devious and inefficient methods, at least by terrestrial standards, to achieve its aims that it is difficult not to believe that coincidence and chance are sometimes responsible for what might be outside intervention. In hospitals especially, where at any moment tens of thou... nds of lives are hanging in the balance, it is hard to see why the help s   d be so arbitrary or so obscure in its pattern. Certainly the way in which a near-tragedy was averted in Chorley hospital in 1968 makes one suspect that if there are benevolent powers, and if they do not wish to be misunderstood, they might use a more direct approach. But perhaps their reasons and methods are too complex for mere humans to comprehend.

Mrs Pauline Gittins, a nursery nurse, with a sister and a staff nurse, was on night duty in November 1968 in the maternity wing, which occupied the whole of one corridor branching off, and quite separate from, the rest of the hospital. The two main wards were full with about 18 patients; there were 14 newly-born babies in the nursery; the side and labour wards were empty. It was very much a routine, uneventful night, with no births imminent and no cases demanding particular attention, so that between one and two in the morning, when life is at its lowest ebb, the three nurses were in the kitchen, the warmest and most comfortable room. The sister was reading a book; Pauline Gittins was skipping through a magazine, and the staff nurse was stretched out in an armchair, her eyes closed, but like the others, her senses acute for the slightest sound that might indicate that help was needed.

Suddenly all three, with that instinctive reaction that perhaps makes people nurses, or which perhaps they acquire in training, were tense:

Mrs Pauline Gittins.

the door of No 1 ward, which made a distinctive creaking noise, opened. A moment later the flip-flopping of someone wearing backless slippers shuffled past the kitchen door. There was no cause for alarm or even any action, as all of the patients were ambulant, and if the nurses had considered it at all they would have assumed that someone had gone to the bathroom or toilet. But when a few seconds later Pauline realised that the toilet door, which also had a highly individual squeal, had not made the slightest sound, she put her magazine down, noting automatically that the other two were also alert. The night sister, in a tone that excluded herself from the short list asked, 'Who's going to check?' and Pauline, as the most junior, accepted her inevitable role.

There was no one in the bathroom or toilets and in the two wards all eighteen patients were deeply asleep—Pauline went to each bed individually to make sure. She checked the labour and side wards in case someone had, half asleep, made a mistake, but all were silent and deserted. Returning very puzzled down the corridor she decided that as she was there she would make a routine check as she passed the nursery, and once inside the door a sense outside herself made her realise that there was something wrong, even before a faint sound from one corner sent her scurrying across the room. Here a two-day old baby had vomited its food and was in the last stage of suffocation. Desperately she cleared the air passages—there was not even time to call the sister—and at last the frail body recovered.

Some time later, when she was satisfied that the child had completely recovered, she was describing what had happened to her two colleagues in the kitchen: suddenly, in a brief pause, as if it had been worrying her, the staff nurse asked, 'Who had gone to the toilet?' For the first time Pauline realised that there had been no one: the door, the footsteps they had all three heard so clearly could not possibly have been caused by a human agency.

Unfortunately, in the steady stream of life that passed through her nights on the maternity ward, Pauline does not remember the baby's name. It would be interesting to have at least the slightest clue whether it was an outside power that saved its life, or whether the mother, though deeply asleep, had in some supernatural way realised the danger and had sent part of her spiritual self to the rescue. But there were three things of which the very experienced nurses were certain: that they did not mistake the sounds; that they could not have been made by any human, and that unless they had occurred the child would almost certainly have died.

Mrs Pauline Gittins, Preston, Lancashire

'Dressed in Victorian clothes, she dashed into the path of a heavy lorry.'

Victorian Ghost Child

It is difficult for anyone setting out to invent a ghost experience to get away from the traditional haunting patterns. Behaviour, dress, appearance and time of the day all fall into a relatively few stereotyped forms so that accounts of headless coachmen, grey ladies, hooded monks and galloping horses at the stroke of midnight need to be investigated with special care, though of course they may well be completely sincere. But the report which has the immediate ring of a genuine experience tends to be the one in which the manifestation is unexpected in all respects— like the one that Elizabeth Bain saw in the village of Mitchell in

Cornwall, and later on the A30 road between Bodmin and Penzance.

In the late summer of 1965 Mrs Bain, a very experienced driver who in her job as a representative travelled many thousands of miles every year in the south-west, was passing through Mitchell in the early afternoon of a warm, sunny day. In the middle of the main street, as is inevitable in the holiday season, the traffic came to a halt. Trapped as she was, Mrs Bain happened to notice a girl aged about nine skipping out of one of the deliberately 'quaint' old shops (Mrs Bain now wonders whether in reality it did really have any existence). She was dressed in what appeared to be Victorian clothes, with a knee-length dress of heavy navy blue material, a starched white pinafore with pleats, black boots and dark stockings. Her curled golden hair was fastened at the side with a bow, and she carried some kind of sweet on a stick.

Mild surprise and faint interest turned immediately to horror as the child, apparently oblivious of the fact that the whole stream of traffic had suddenly accelerated away, dashed across the road without pausing or looking up, straight into the path of a heavy lorry immediately in front of Elizabeth's car. Mrs Bain, with reactions conditioned by years of driving, braked instantly, but the lorry made not the slightest hesitation. It roared away, increasing in speed every moment, and when it was well clear, Elizabeth could see that the driver had made no attempt to avoid the child—because she did not exist. She was certainly not on either side of the street, but that was not surprising because if she had been human there could have been no possible way of avoiding a collision.

Very shaken and upset, Elizabeth Bain was brought back to reality by the imperious hooting of the drivers behind her, and putting her car into gear, she drove on. She had seen accidents before, and in her career had been involved in many near misses, but never before had she felt her reactions and anticipations been so incredibly acute and her instincts so sharp as when she hurried on to Penzance that afternoon. When she reached Hayle, some 31 miles beyond Mitchell, suddenly and without any signal a very large van immediately ahead of her swung left into a narrow opening, masking as it did so a lorry which, seizing what it assumed to be a momentary break in the traffic, shot out into the main road. Normally a collision would have been inevitable, but Elizabeth's instinct was so acute that without the situation really registering on her conscious mind, she accelerated violently, swerved desperately to the right, and by a miracle scraped round the front of the still-moving lorry to safety.

Almost before she had time to comprehend what had happened she saw again the apparition of the little girl she had so mysteriously witnessed an hour earlier: the golden head and the upper half of the body appeared directly in front of her, as if the child were a passenger in the

'The girl, now smiling, reappeared as a reflection on the windscreen.'

back of her car being reflected in the windscreen. The image lasted only two or three seconds, but was unmistakably clear: the sweet on a stick was still clutched in her hand but her face, previously flat and expressionless, was now smiling. The rest of the journey to Penzance was completely uneventful. The unprecedented acuteness of Mrs Bain's senses and reactions disappeared and, as the danger for which she had been supernaturally prepared was now past, she felt utterly relaxed.

Since then Elizabeth Bain has tried logically and objectively to find out why the experience should have happened: she has searched her history in an effort to remember if she has ever come into contact with any child resembling the one she saw in Mitchell, without any success. She admits that in all her long driving life this is the nearest she has ever come to an accident, and is confident that had she not been warned, even in this vague and indirect way, she would almost certainly have been severely injured, if not killed.

Elizabeth Bain, Plymouth

The Prophecy of the Bed

The world of the supernatural spreads far beyond the traditional realm of earth-bound spirits, and our language often seems inadequate in its vocabulary. None of our usual words such as 'ghost', 'haunting', 'apparition' can describe the manifestations that sometimes fore-shadow events to come. 'Precognition' smacks of Zenner cards and seems far too cold and clinical for the intensely moving and personal experience that Penny Watson went through in 1976.

In December 1975 Penny Wing married Julian Watson who at 26 was two years her senior, and in April 1976 Julian, who was a chef, got a job in Penny's home town of Looe. They decided that for the short time they would be there they would stay with her parents who had prepared a room for them. But as so often happens, the initial euphoria of marriage had dulled, and feeling that the difficult transition to a deeper relationship of affection and understanding would perhaps be hindered by living with 'in-laws' Julian decided to take temporary lodgings for himself in the town while Penny stayed with her parents.

A few days after parting Penny went to bed as usual: she says that she was not tired, but no doubt the emotional episode left her in a tense state; she lay open-eyed in the tiny pink room staring at the ceiling lit by the glow from the bedside lamp. Suddenly she felt that the bed was moving up and down slightly: she knew that this was ridiculous, and recalling her thoughts from their wanderings she brought them to focus on the present. With her senses taut she sat up in bed and coldly and logically confirmed by both feeling and sight that the bed was indeed rising and falling rhythmically like a boat in a gentle swell. Then almost at once Penny realised that it was not a wave motion, but a breathing . . . rise . . . pause . . . fall . . . pause . . . rise . . . To corroborate further the impression, there began—quietly at first, but gradually intensifying—the sound of air being drawn in, and then expelled. Terrifyingly, this became increasingly laboured and wheezing like an asthmatic or bronchitic struggling for breath. Penny leaped from the bed and stood watching it under the light: the motion and the torturous sounds died away, but the moment she lay down again the sickening movements and the agonised gasping resumed.

With fear, dismay and incredulity Penny sat up and looked round the little pink room, and at the almost new divan which her father had recently bought at an auction sale rising and falling beneath her. She and Julian had slept in the bed before many times, and apart from being a little cramped for his exceptional height, it had always been what it purported to be—a normal divan. Whatever this frightening experience was she had no idea, but she was determined to see it through—and at this point there came a sharp ringing in her ears which almost at once turned into a high-pitched hum like an electric motor running at speed. The hum whined up to a crescendo, and as it became almost unbearable in pitch and intensity, there was a blinding flash of light which for an instant turned the pink into a shadowless glare of brilliant white, and then faded.

Sound and motion ceased abruptly, and completely shattered, Penny fled to her twin brother's room. Here, huddled in blankets she poured out her story, and heard in return that her father too had slept on the divan, and like her he had felt a heaving motion. This became so violent that he was thrown on the floor in the night, an incident which had been the source of much family hilarity ever since. Penny, not un-naturally, refused to sleep in the bed again: five days later she was summoned urgently to Freedom Fields Hospital where Julian, who had been thrown from the pillion seat of a motor cycle, lay critically ill with chest injuries. The terrible apprehension for his safety as she entered the hospital turned to horror as she entered the little ward where her husband lay inert, kept alive only by a respirator pumping air into lungs that could no longer do it for themselves. The bellows rose and fell, mechanically forcing some semblance of life into the shattered chest: his tormented breath wheezed harshly at each exhala-tion. It was a sickening re-enactment of the motions and sounds she herself had experienced only a few days earlier.

To the amazement of the doctors Julian lived for two weeks in this no-man's-land of existence, fighting to hold on to the world he had enjoyed so much. When not heavily sedated to ease his pain his mind was conscious and logical, and though speech was impossible he could communicate in simple terms by blinking. But even his tremendous willpower was not enough to keep him alive.

Penny writes: 'I am convinced that he has not left this earth as it was all he knew. Though he has not materialised there are lots of things that suggest to me that he is still around, transformed into thoughts and energy—things we cannot see.' The bed, with its awful prophetic powers, was burnt immediately.

Penny Watson, Plymouth

The Black Dog

For well over a thousand years there has been a tradition in much of Northern Europe of a phantom black dog that roams the darkness, generally as a harbinger of death or ill fortune to those who see it. Like

'She went to call the dog when, in front of her eyes, it disappeared.'

the Wild Hunt of Odin, this is generally considered to be a fragment of folk memory stemming from the old, dark religion of the Germanic tribes in their sinister forest homelands, but the frequency with which the dog at least is reported spontaneously from all over Britain by people who are quite unaware of the legends makes one wonder whether the facts really did come first, and not the story.

In 1970 Barbara Myatt, an artist, and her family spent a holiday in an isolated cottage on the remote island of Hoy in the Orkneys. The building, which had once been the lodge of Melsetter House, still had no electricity but had been partially modernised by the addition of a small, new wing housing the kitchen and bathroom. The original back door now led to an enclosed corridor from which the new rooms opened and at the end of which a further door led to the garden.

One evening after Barbara had put her daughter to bed, she picked up a portable oil lamp and went towards the kitchen to boil a kettle of water for a drink when her husband returned. As she stepped through the old back door into the corridor she was surprised to see a large black collie rush forward towards her—she says that she noticed particularly the way its hair curled along its back—and assumed that the outer door had been left open so that a local farmer's dog had got in. As the animal did not seem to be aggressive, she went to call it, when in front of her eyes it faded from sight. Barbara was too astonished to be afraid, but a moment or two later, when she had checked that the outside door was indeed securely fastened and that there were no open windows through which the creature could have entered, terror began to shiver along her spine.

When her husband returned shortly afterwards he tried to persuade her that the whole thing had been a trick of light and shadows from the unaccustomed and flickering oil lamp, but experiments failed to produce anything vaguely resembling the animal. In any case, Barbara knew that the dog had been clear and definite, unmistakably real, and that no shadow could have given the fine detail of the hair.

Although Barbara's daughter complained of strange noises, nothing else abnormal was experienced until the morning the family was due to return to their home on the mainland. Then, in the bright sunshine soon after dawn on an utterly still day, everyone was awakened by a tremendous crash which seemed to vibrate through the solid stone walls of the old building. As the reverberations died away a great stillness followed: no explanation was ever found, in spite of a thorough search of the house and outside. It may have been coincidence, but Mrs Myatt's mother died very suddenly a few weeks later.

Barbara Myatt, Halkirk, Caithness

Family Ghosts

The Living Ghost

An instinctive fear of the shadows of the dead is quite irrational, for as the physical body no longer exists there would seem to be little danger of material harm. A phantom of a living person, however, should perhaps cause deeper concern, for there is still a living power related to it which might be capable of real injury.

The Laity children of Redruth—Lionel, Douglas and Beatrice—had a very unhappy childhood. Beatrice speaks, not in a spirit of hatred, but with sadness and bewilderment, of her mother's 'vicious way of life, both in thought and action' and of her father, an ex-naval man of a hard, earlier school, unbending and unforgiving. Weakness to him was the ultimate sin and crime: if in the constant recriminations and corrections one of his children cried, or if one showed any sympathy with the other, the punishment fell more heavily and more bitterly.

In the difficult years of her early teens the only compassion Beatrice felt at home was from her brothers, especially the eldest, Lionel, who had blazed the path of misery and tried as best he could to soften the

Lionel, Douglas and Beatrice Laity at the time of the war. Mrs Davey's locket contains a photo of her eldest brother.

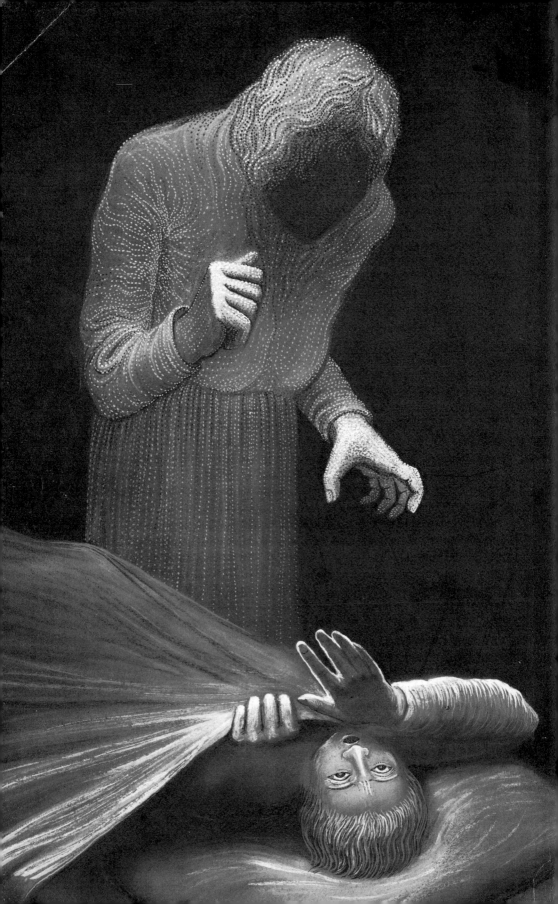

blows he knew so well. One tiny gesture in particular became the symbol of this deep understanding between brother and sister: when Mr Laity bullied his daughter hoping that he could force her into tears so that his fullest fury could be unleashed, Lionel would sense when his sister was at breaking point and·manoeuvring so that his father could not see, he would gently touch her on the crown of her head and let his hand slide down to the nape of her neck, just once. Instantly Beatrice knew that she was not alone, not taking the weight of her father's anger on her own shoulders, but in some way sharing it.

In 1939 the family moved to Plymouth and when the war broke out the two boys immediately joined the navy so that Beatrice was left alone to face her misery. She was just 14 when the whole of her frail world collapsed: the brother she worshipped was killed in what must have been one of the cruellest tricks that fate played during the war. Lionel's ship, HMS *Registan*, anchored late on the night of 27 May 1941 just outside Falmouth harbour at the end of a patrol, awaiting first light to enter, when a single German plane dropped a single bomb which fell straight down the funnel, exploding in the very heart of the vessel. Everyone in the area was torn to fragments.

Beatrice was distraught: her parents, perhaps to hide their own feelings, were unable or unwilling to show any sympathy or under-standing. Beatrice's grief and emotion built up dangerously in her isolation: she rejected her deep belief in religion, and daily the peace of extinction grew more appealing. One night when the call for self-destruction had become irresistible, she suddenly felt the pressure of a light hand smoothing her head from crown to nape, and she knew that from somewhere her brother had come to comfort her for the last time. Only this time it was not tears he was blocking, but death itself. From that momentary touch her hatred and bitterness vanished: she could face the lesser but still staggering blow of her second brother's death in HMS *Dorsetshire* a few months later with resignation.

But time moved on, and healed. The war ended and in 1949 Beatrice married, at last finding peace and happiness in her husband and children. The nightmares of the past seemed to be just nightmares, and if they did not disappear on waking, they could at least be put into perspective. Then in 1961 came the experience that brought the black tides of the past flooding back: Beatrice had been deeply asleep, but found herself instantly awake with her senses preternaturally clear and keen. There, standing silent and ominous at the foot of her bed was the grey form of an elderly woman with distinctive bushy hair and outline but with her face veiled and unrecognisable in what seemed deliberate shadow. Although there was no sound and no visible expression,

'The being was filled with an unbelievable hatred towards her.'

Beatrice knew that the being was filled with an unbelievable hatred towards her—a malevolence which intensified as the apparition moved slowly and with undisguised menace towards the head of the bed.

Beatrice called out, 'Who are you? What do you want?' and as the figure moved inexorably and soundlessly on, she desperately invoked her deep religious belief to dispel the vision. Whether it was this, or whether it was because she leaned towards her husband's bed to waken him, the phantom slowly faded. 'I knew', says Beatrice, 'that I had never done anything in my life to warrant such hatred from another human being, and I admit that for many nights I was afraid to go to sleep.' But slowly the most pressing dread faded, though the intensity of her fear had burned the image with absolute clarity into her consciousness. In 1969 Beatrice's father died, and though relations had in no way mellowed over the years, her mother, lonely and elderly came to live with the family. Yet this, it seemed, and the three grandchildren, seemed only to add fresh fuel to the old lady's blazing fire of antagonism and bitterness.

One night in November 1970 Beatrice woke to hear a faint shuffling sound and a moment later a grey shape of a figure slid past the frosted glass of her bedroom door. Instantly the memory of that fearful phantom of nine years earlier leaped from the past as Beatrice slipped from bed into the darkened corridor. The landing was completely empty and silent: she hurried apprehensively to the door of her daughter's bedroom which was open, and there, in the faint glow from outside she saw with horror the same grey shape looming motionless and menacing at the foot of the bed. The outline, the bushy hair and the slight stoop of age were identical with that other apparition, and with awful apprehension Beatrice instinctively stretched out her hand to ward it off.

But more terrifyingly than if she had encountered nothing, her outstretched hand touched a solid human body: in panic she switched on the dim night light and saw her mother standing there, her eyes blazing with a hatred that transcended even that of the other phantom. In utter silence, but with her eyes fixed with intense malevolence on her daughter, the old woman shuffled back to her room. Beatrice was so distressed and so physically afraid of what might happen that she saw her doctor the following morning: on his advice her mother was sent to stay with her own sister some distance away. Here she died six months later.

'I know', says Beatrice, 'that the "person" I saw years earlier was not the ghost of a dead person as I had thought, but some kind of presence of a future conflict with my own mother.' She wonders now just why that apparition should have appeared in 1962, not long after the birth of her daughter. Was it resentment so powerful that the shadow could be projected? Was it a warning of what might have happened on that night in 1970? Or was there some other reason for the strange spirit wandering?

Mrs B M Davey, Plymouth

'And Now You'll Believe in Ghosts . . .'

In 1975 Diane Glaze and her three children returned from Malta where her marriage had broken up, to live with her sister. Here she was introduced to Isa Samat, a Malaysian studying dietetics at Aberdeen: in the next six months acquaintance turned to love, and in September 1976, as soon as Diane's divorce was absolute, the couple married. Shortly before this, however, they set up house together. One night in late July 1976 Diane woke, noticed that it was 2am, and despite the hot summer she experienced, rather than felt, a sensation of chill that seemed to be of the spirit rather than of the body. Almost immediately out of the darkness there came an inexplicable feeling of panic. she looked up and to her amazement saw a tall, gaunt woman standing near the door of the bedroom. The room was, she knew, in pitch blackness, but the figure seemed lit by some internal illumination. In an instant the details burnt themselves into her mind, sharpened by fear: the grey hair drawn back into an untidy bunch, but straggling loose at the sides; the yellow and grey dress in a rough diamond check pattern; the sleeves rolled up to the elbows and the pale brown of the face and arms.

Diane closed her eyes to make sure they had been open before and then shook her head to convince herself that she was awake. Again she opened her eyes hoping that reason would dispel the frightening vision but to her horror the figure had moved along the side of the bed and was very close to her: it held out two arms that seemed little more than bones tightly encased in dark, ridged skin with talon-like fingers. As Diane shrank back against the bed head the hard thin fingers seemed to encircle her neck: she had the sensation of them tightening, shutting off the air to her lungs. Terrified, Diane clutched at the throttling wrists and, sickened by the icy coldness and putty-like feel of the flesh, she pulled for her very life. But she might as well have tugged at the girders of a steel bridge. As the inexorable grip tightened, and as the forearms pressed more heavily on her chest, a horrible gurgling came from Diane's throat. In a mind paralysed by the terror of the unknown and the dread of death, she prayed in the one lucid corner of her brain that the frantic sounds would waken Isa, but he slept on undisturbed.

Then suddenly, relief: the fingers relaxed, the arms dropped back as

the old woman with a sardonic sneer turned away. Although Diane is not certain she actually heard sounds she knew the woman was communicating over and over again. 'And now you'll believe in ghosts, and now you'll believe in ghosts.' Diane began to scream hysterically: the old woman hurried towards the door as if to make a normal exit, and then suddenly faded. Isa leaped from sleep and snapped on the light. Diane sat up clutching her neck which, like her chest was sore for days afterwards, and babbled incoherently.

When she had calmed down and looked at the experience logically, she wondered whether the apparition could have been of the old widow who had occupied the flat for forty years and had died there. But gradually she became aware that Isa was not following her speculations: he was sitting with a strange, far-off expression as if he was peering with disbelief into his past. Only reluctantly could he be persuaded to talk, perhaps because he did not wish to open himself to ridicule, but more probably because he did not really want to believe it himself. Again and again he asked Diane to describe the figure to him, and then said simply, 'That was my grandmother.' The only detail which did not tally perfectly was the dress: the old lady had indeed usually worn material of yellow and grey, but the patterns were invariably floral, not check.

Isa's parents it seemed, had split up when he was two months old, and from that age he had been brought up by his 'grandparents' in Molucca—they were in fact a couple who had adopted his own mother as a child. The grandmother had been a powerful personality, dominating the family: she had indulged her grandson, but at the same time had been insanely jealous and possessive of him as she was of her own husband. Grandfather had scarcely a life to call his own: he was questioned endlessly if he was a few minutes later from work than usual, and was followed even if he went to a neighbour's for a chat.

Grandmother died when Isa was six but though he was so young her influence was dominant through his childhood and adolescence. His grandfather, still alive in Malaysia, says that he constantly feels his long-dead wife about him, watching, checking, prying, and that he frequently dreams of her standing beside Isa's bed, stroking her grandson's hair. But that is the old lady's home ground. It seems now that she may have found her way across half the world when she felt her authority and influence challenged. But perhaps she was satisfied by what she saw. Perhaps she found in Diane someone who could take her place as protector and companion to her beloved Isa, for never since that night has there been any hint of another visitation.

A strange postscript to Diane Samat's story occurred in January

'The hard thin fingers seemed to encircle her neck.'

1977 when Margaret Collins, a reporter from BBC Radio Aberdeen went to her home to record, in the haunted bedroom, her experiences. The interview went perfectly but when the tape was played back in the studio it was quite unusable because of an uncanny undulating noise in the background. The recorder had been checked both before and after the interview, and a second attempt with the same machine in a different room was faultless.

Mrs D Samat, Aberdeen

In Another Country

Of all English towns perhaps Coggeshall in Essex with its magnificent timbered and pargetted medieval houses is the most English of all, and understandably draws many thousands of visitors every year. By its very antiquity it should be, and by repute is, the home of many traditional ghosts and legends, yet the strangest of the supernatural reports comes not from the ancient buildings whose stories, like their timbers, are warped and twisted by time, but from a small, semi-detached cottage on the outskirts, which is occupied by a vivacious young American and her English husband. How Gay Agnes from a small mining town in Ohio should meet Mick Brock, a farm worker from East Anglia is a tale almost as strange as Gay's supernatural experiences.

Gay was the youngest of three children and very deeply attached to her mother, partly because she was the 'baby' and partly because of an indefinable and strange bond that seemed to link them in character and spirit. Then in 1969 when Gay was seventeen her happy and relatively uneventful life was shattered by the sudden death of her mother: her vivacity collapsed into intense misery and for most of each morning she would lie wakeful in bed, numb with wretchedness and with all desire to live dead inside her. Her father, her elder sister and two small coloured boys her mother had adopted were left to manage as well as they could.

About a month after the funeral Gay was lying in her bed at about 11 o'clock in the morning, trying to keep her mind blank because of the anguish that filled it, when she was aware almost without registering it consciously, of a white hand feeling round the slightly-open door. A second later her mother was sitting on the bed. Gay did not see her

'Her arms encircled what seemed a living, solid figure.'

42

come in, nor any connection with the hand: one moment there was nothing, the next the bed springs were sinking and creaking as if with the weight of a normal human being. Then the familiar and characteristic smell she had always associated with her mother filled her nostrils.

Gay says that she was not afraid: it was the past month that had been the unreality, and this was a lifelong normality. Her mother was alive, dressed in her favourite red and black dress, comforting her for a grief that was for the instant pointless. Gay sat up and embraced her mother instinctively: her arms encircled what seemed a living, solid figure. The flesh was soft and warm, and not the cold, inhuman wax Gay had touched in the funeral parlour.

Her mother gently moved back, and speaking sadly, used the name she used only in times of intense emotion: 'Gay Agnes, shouldn't you be out there looking after them?' Then, as strangely as it had come, the weight lifted from the bed and the figure was just not there any more. The whole episode, Gay says, lasted about sixty seconds. She got up and set about the house with an urgency she had not felt before in her life, and hurried to the basement to put laundry in the machine. Some time later she returned to take it out and glancing casually round the room waiting for the cycle to end, she saw, to her utter amazement, the red and black dress in which the apparition had appeared an hour earlier. Reluctant lest this be an insubstantial shadow, she went slowly towards it, hesitantly put out a hand—but the dress was material enough, and as she picked it up there came again that rich evocative odour as if it had just been taken off. Deeply moved she telephoned her father at work, who said that it was impossible—the dress, like all his wife's belongings had been packed away in trunks in the loft weeks before to avoid the sad memories they recalled.

Almost seven years later, married and coping with a husband, her two adopted brothers and an unfamiliar life in rural England, Gay had a dream that was so intense and so sharp-edged in clarity that she was instantly awake. A minute later she was pouring out in detail to a sleepy husband how she had been kneeling beside a grave of a kind fairly common in England but rare in Ohio. It consisted of a rectangle of marble kerbstone filled with marble chippings, and a headstone whose lettering she could not distinguish. In the dream she was picking up handfuls of the gravel and letting them trickle through her fingers into little heaps. It seemed so trivial that it was difficult to see why it had made such an impression, yet for the next two months those few moments in the cemetery kept re-enacting themselves spontaneously in her mind as if something was trying constantly to remind her of the details.

One afternoon in mid-August 1976 she left the path she normally used to cross the churchyard of St Peter and took a short cut at the rear

Mrs Gay Brock at the grave of Nell Osborne Coggeshall.

of the building: suddenly she was brought to a physical and mental halt by the sight of the grave she had seen first in her vivid dream and had recalled so often in her household chores. It was ill-kept, overgrown and with the lettering on the headstone decipherable only with difficulty. But when she knelt, as she had in her dream and rubbed away the lichen, she was staggered to read:

<blockquote>
In sweet memory of
Nell Osborne
Wife of Henry Coggeshall of New York
Died in London, England
Jan 16 1927
'Out of the rolling ocean, the crowd'
</blockquote>

If the dream of the unknown grave had been persistent, it was nothing compared with its impact now that she had found it. The name Nell Osborne went round and round in her brain, especially at night when she lay sleepless, and she felt that she was being asked to do something on behalf of someone else. The insistent demand became so intense that after a few days Gay was forced to see her doctor, but the inevitable tranquilisers did nothing to still that compelling request.

Then suddenly Gay knew: she withdrew the few pounds she had in savings, bought a pot and a heather plant which the assistant told her would remain always green, and hurried to the churchyard. She weeded the grave, tidied the chippings and placed the little shrub in the centre. Everything now seemed all right: the urgent voice was silent. But often Gay wonders how Mrs Coggeshall of New York came to be buried in Coggeshall, England: and whether her shadow, far from home, neglected and forgotten, had reached out to another exile for help.

Gay Brock, Essex

The Phantom of Love

A few years after the Second World War Diana Belfield, the daughter of a family living in Bath, married an Austrian, Frederic Ludwig. One evening in 1954 when the Ludwigs' son Carl was four years old, his mother was tucking him up as usual to sleep and for some trivial reason she no longer remembers moved the chair that stood at the head of the bed to the other side of the room. Immediately Carl said: 'Mummy, don't do that—that's where the lady always sits.' Like most mothers, Diana was well aware that pre-school children often people their world with fantasy figures, and more to humour the boy at the critical bedtime stage than anything else, she asked about 'the lady'. Although at the beginning of the conversation Diana made only an occasional non-committal interjection, she was brought up suddenly when Carl talked of a tall slender lady with green rings in her ears and 'long feets'. Diana stood motionless with an emotion mixed of astonishment and disbelief while the boy babbled on with a minute description of the 'lady' who sat in the chair, held his hand, but never spoke. 'I think she loves me', he concluded.

As soon as she could without betraying her intense feelings, Diana left the room trying to come to terms with what her son, in all innocence, had said, for he had given her a precise and unmistakable description of her grandmother, to whom she had been devoted, and

'He talked of the 'lady' who sat in the chair, held his hand, but never spoke. "I think she loves me", he concluded.'

46

who had died in 1937 aged 67. Mrs Priest, upright, dignified and beautiful had invariably worn jade earrings, and as a result of a series of operations on her feet had been compelled to wear unusually long surgical shoes. She had said towards the end of her life that if only she could see her grand-daughter married happily with children she could die happily. Unfortunately she did not live to see her wish fulfilled, passing away when Diana was only 17.

Although she was then expecting her second child, Mrs Ludwig had not been consciously thinking more than usual of her grandmother recently. For some days she wondered how she could prove to herself that she had not distorted a simple childhood fantasy into a detailed description of her grandmother. Then searching deliberately through the sentimental family photographs, she found a picture of her grand-mother taken shortly before her death. She left it lying, apparently casually, on the dining room table. In the morning, unobserved but observing, she watched Carl at play, pottering round the house. At length he saw the picture, picked it up, stared hard, and then smiling delightedly said, 'Mummy, that's the lady who sits by me.' He then put it back where he had found it and resumed his game as if the whole episode had been as trivial and as normal as the recognition of an aeroplane, an elephant or Father Christmas in one of his picture books. From that day the 'visits' began to dwindle: Diana made some oblique but leading references at bedtime for several days, but the boy seemed unconcerned not deliberately uncommunicative, but merely behaving as if the subject were no longer relevant.

It is difficult to suggest a reason for the manifestation at this specific time. Can it be that the imminent arrival of the second baby, in the event a girl, had some bearing on the issue? Once again, the facts are so carefully documented and corroborated by Carl himself, that one can only puzzle on the apparent illogicality and arbitrariness of the supernatural.

Mrs D Ludwig, Bath

Bonds Between Life and Death

Grandmothers, it is said, have all the delights of parenthood without the responsibilities, and there is no doubt that a very strong bond often exists between old and young. It may be that in these days of scattered families the actual physical presence of a grandmother is less significant than it used to be but it takes more than a century or two of mobility and separation to alter the emotional ties and feelings, and this may well be the drive behind a number of psychic experiences reported with great detail from several parts of the country.

In 1966 Brigit Sanderson married her second husband, James Thompson, and settled in a flat in Dundee. James was the youngest of a large family and though his mother had died when he was only eight, and she in her mid-40s, he was very deeply attached to her memory. In the cold spring of 1970 Brigit had a son and as the only fireplace in the flat was in the sitting room, she and her husband decided to sleep there temporarily on a bed-settee with the baby in his pram. One night early in May Brigit felt unnaturally restless: she read beside her sleeping husband until the early hours of the morning when, although she did not feel in the least tired, she put out the light. But in the darkness the strange sensation of unease and expectancy only increased, and she sat up with the intention of making herself a cup of tea.

As she eased herself slowly upright she was suddenly shocked to see in the light from the street lamp outside and the still-glowing fire, the vague shape of a woman standing at the foot of the bed. Almost immediately the shape became more sharply defined and opaque and Brigit could distinguish clearly the long white dress with sleeves to the wrist, and black hair hanging down to the shoulders. As the face emerged more and more distinctly, it was obviously that of a middle-aged woman. The initial fear passed quickly and it was almost with curiosity that Brigit watched, though apprehension flooded back when the apparition crossed the room to the pram, bent over it and stretched out a hand towards the baby's face. Brigit has no idea how long the phantom stayed in vision, but it was certainly long enough for her to collect her senses completely—and then to doubt them—so that she looked critically round the room to see whether any shadows cast by the light through the window could in any way create the image she saw. There was nothing to account for it, and when she was convinced that it was indeed a ghost, she roused her husband: and as so often happens, the figure faded.

James assumed that his wife had been dreaming and the matter was dismissed. But the following night there came the same sequence—the strangely disquieting restlessness, the black-haired apparition that crossed to the pram and looked closely at the baby. When James was awakened this time, he was annoyed and insisted that the next night they move back to the bedroom where the baby was put in his usual cot. The pram was, however, left in the sitting room, and as far as Brigit was concerned, the night was its normal, uneventful self.

But the relief that the strange appearance may after all have been a dream or a figment of imagination was shattered at breakfast time when Brigit's nine-year-old daughter by a previous marriage said: 'You didn't half scare me last night, mum. I was going to the bathroom in the dark and I saw you standing by the pram in the sitting room without moving or speaking. I wondered what you were up to.' When Brigit asked how she knew it was her mother, the girl replied, 'Well, you had got your white nightdress on, and your hair was down.' She added that when she had come back from the bathroom she had slipped into the sitting room to find out what her mother was doing, but found the place empty and assumed that she had gone back to bed. Brigit did not deny that she had been to the room during the night to avoid frightening the girl, nor did she tell her that as she had washed her hair the previous evening it had been in rollers as she slept. James said nothing while his step-daughter was there but as soon as she had gone he apologised for his disbelief.

As far as the Thompsons know the apparition did not appear again, but a strange echo took place a month later. They were visiting James' brother in Dundee, and were looking through a collection of family photographs. 'This' said her husband, handing Brigit a snapshot of a woman in her 40s, 'is my mother'. Brigit looked with incredulity at the face and other details of the head-and-shoulders portrait: they were identical with those of the figure she had seen standing by the baby's pram. She said nothing, but for the rest of the evening she felt too disturbed to join in the general conversation. On the way home James asked her what had been the matter, and rather reluctantly she told him that the woman in the photograph, and the apparition were one and the same. James now no longer just believed—he understood.

Name supplied, Dundee

These We Have Known

The Silent Summoner

From the very beginning Christian religious leaders have realised that trying to reconcile belief in a conscious future life with a second marriage raises deep emotional and theological problems. Although nominally settled by the New Testament ruling, the issue is still acute to many very devout people who have had two happy marriages and who find it difficult to come to terms with the situation. One hopes that there is a satisfactory answer, for in these days when half a dozen spouses, let alone two, are common, there could be some agonising moments in another world. Mr Ben Chicken, of Ushaw Moor, near Durham, has had the realities of the situation brought home with a force that few people in that position have to face.

In 1937 John Mahan of Sherbrun Road, Durham died of bronchitis, leaving a 36-year-old widow, Jane, and five children—a daunting prospect in the depressed north-east of the 1930s. In order to survive Mrs Mahan adopted the traditional solution of taking a lodger, 27-year-old Ben Chicken. The result was inevitable: loneliness, economics and purely practical difficulties brought the two together. They were married at a register office in 1938 and again at St Joseph's Catholic church five years later. 'It was not love then,' says Mr Chicken, 'just convenience. Real love came later.' He became deeply attached to the children—two boys and three girls—whom he regarded as his own.

Life in these circumstances would have been hard at any time, but the material privations of wartime austerity made it extremely difficult, yet this only drew the family closer. When in 1942 the second son, John Robert Mahan, joined the forces, the world seemed balanced on the knife-edge of hope and fear. In mid-June 1944 with the excitement and dread of the invasion of Europe the universal topic, Ben Chicken dreamed, or perhaps saw—he is not sure which—the figure of a perfectly ordinary working man in modern clothing standing silently beside the bed, staring hard at the occupants. The apparition stayed long enough for Ben to register every detail of face and dress, and then vanished.

The incident made such a deep impression on him that he poured out a minute description over breakfast, not noticing the growing tension and fear in his wife's face. It was only when he had finished that Jane stammered out that he had given an incredibly accurate and complete picture of her first husband, whom Ben had never seen, and of whom she had no photograph to prove her point. The couple parted that morning puzzled and apprehensive—an apprehension that was tragically justified later in the day when the dreaded telegram arrived saying curtly and officially that John Robert had been killed in action. For the next six months, Mr Chicken says, the apparition appeared regularly, always silent and motionless. Perhaps Mr Mahan, with the best of motives, was trying to comfort Jane for the loss of their son but to Ben it seemed that the motives could be more sinister and possessive. 'I ached', he says, 'to wake her and tell her I loved her. I even got jealous and asked who she would come to in the hereafter.'

Slowly the vision became less frequent, and by the end of 1944 had ceased altogether: the war ended, life improved, and over the years the children grew up, left home and married. The middle-aged couple moved to the house at Ushaw Moor where Mr Chicken still lives, and as they grew closer the dreams of 1944 slipped into a dusty corner of memory as a mysterious but unhappy nightmare. Then in mid-1973 time collapsed, and the awful apprehension of almost twenty years earlier flooded back as once again the incorporeal Mr Mahan stood beside the bed as he had before, silent and ominous. For several weeks Ben prayed in vain that his sleep that night would be free of the preying figure, which he knew on waking presaged some disaster. The memory of his earlier miseries of loneliness turned his life into a blur of unhappiness as he waited for the blow he knew was coming.

So, it was not entirely unexpected when he returned home from the pit one evening to find his wife collapsed on the floor. He helped her to bed, but knew inside that the messenger's purpose was all too obvious. Jane lingered, speechless, for three weeks before she died. Emptiness settled like a pall on the house in Chestnut Grove: even the dream figure, its purpose accomplished, disappeared. Age dulls, and time

Ben Chicken.

heals, but the shock was as keen as ever when in September 1975 Ben found the terrible apparition once more at his bedside. The figure was so vivid, says Ben, that I could not believe it was a vision. This time the emotion he experienced was not so much fear as anger and confusion: what more could this form that had hounded him for almost 30 years want from him? Mr Chicken did not have to wait long for an answer: within a few hours of the figure fading his step daughter came with the news that the youngest son, Vincent Mahan, had collapsed over the wheel of the lorry he was driving and had died in hospital.

Ben Chicken not unnaturally lives in dread of the recurring phantom. It seems to Ben there is only one more thing that it can come for. We can only hope that the answer Christ gave to the Sadducces is the true one: 'In the resurrection they will neither marry, nor are given in marriage, but are as the angels of God in Heaven.'

Mr B D Chicken, Durham

To Keep My Treasures Safe

A quarter of a century before Uri Geller's key-bending and watch-stopping experiments of the 1970s Hazel Covington had a similar experience in Coventry.

Hazel's parents went to live at 3 Trensale Avenue, Coventry in the 1930s when she was eight years old. Mr and Mrs Terrill who lived next door at number 5 had no children of their own (though Mrs Terrill had a daughter, then dead, by a previous marriage who had been married to a Mr Evans) and as so often happens, they became very attached to the little girl as she grew up. When his wife died in 1939 Mr Terrill leaned more heavily on Hazel and her parents, for apart from his 'stepson-in-law' his only known relative was an invalid sister of whom he was very fond but whom he could rarely see.

When Hazel married in 1945, property in the badly blitzed city was even more scarce than it was in many other towns in England, and the young couple were delighted when Mr Terrill offered them half of No 5 as a home. Mr Terrill, though well past retirement age, kept on his work as a carpenter partly because as an active man he needed something to occupy his time and partly because he felt that the devastated city needed his skills. The arrangement worked out very well on both practical and personal levels: the Covingtons had the security of a comfortable home, while Mr Terrill had his house looked after, his meals prepared and most important of all, warm human contact. Both sides became even more deeply attached to each other.

Hazel was entrusted with the whole house, though as she was frequently in her parents' home next door Mr Terrill fitted a lock to his bedroom door 'where', he said, 'my treasures are kept.' The key of this, however, was always placed with his ration books and other personal papers in a bureau in the back room so that it was always available if Hazel needed it. The bureau itself was kept locked and its key placed on a special shelf in the kitchen. Unfortunately this happy arrangement was destined not to last: on Friday, 3 November, 1946, Mr Terrill set out for work as usual but was knocked down by a car and died two days later without recovering consciousness. He had previously asked that his stepson-in-law be contacted in the event of his death, and immediately after breakfast on Monday morning—Hazel had just locked the bureau and put its key in the usual place—Mr Covington was about to set out for Mr Evans' house when two women, both strangers, knocked at the door. They said that they were Mr Terrill's relatives and demanded to be taken to his room 'to go through his things'. Assuming that the women would understand the dead man's wishes when they were explained to them, Mr Covington left his wife to deal with them, and hurried off.

But the visitors, far from understanding, became abusive, then aggressive, and demanded angrily to be taken to the old man's rooms. When they were told that the place was locked, they brushed aside all arguments and demanded the key at once. The information that the door key was locked in the bureau incensed them and as Hazel had obviously begun to play for time, the women became desperate, threatening violence. Suddenly catching sight of Mr Terrill's bag of tools on the floor, one of them bent down and snatched out a large chisel, saying that she would break open the bureau if they were not given the key of it. As it was obvious that they fully intended carrying out their threat, Hazel capitulated.

She reached out for the key she had placed on its shelf less than an hour earlier to hand to the red-faced, furious women: she picked it up—and then, though normally a very placid woman, she screamed hysterically. The key, which an hour before had been perfectly intact, was now completely useless: only the ring and upper half of the shank remained in her fingers—the lower half and the wards had been sliced off in a sloping cut as if from a giant's knife and had vanished. The visitors hesitated, thinking that Hazel was merely shouting to attract attention, but the sheer horror on her face must have convinced them that she was not acting. They stood uneasy, uncertain, while Hazel collapsed into a chair staring incredulously at the remains of the key still clasped in her hand, and before anyone could recover from the shock, Mr Covington and Mr Evans returned. The two women were never identified, nor despite an exhaustive search, was the other half of the key ever found: the wards were not in the lock, nor in either of the only two rooms Hazel had been in. Mr Terrill's 'treasures' may have had relatively little intrinsic value, but their sentimental worth, Hazel believes, were great enough for him to use psychic means to prevent them from falling into what he thought were the wrong hands.

Mrs Hazel Covington, Coventry

My Son, My Son

The minor B4567 road from Marlborough to Hungerford follows the valley of the river Kennet eastwards, and where it crosses a spur of the downs at Mildenhall a cutting was made at the top of Rectory Hill to reduce the gradient for horse traffic. For a stretch of about 200 yards the road runs between almost vertical banks some 9 feet high, and it was in this gully that a tragic accident occurred in 1879. The local paper reported:

> A quiet but valuable team of three horses, none of which had ever been known to run away, suddenly started from an unknown cause and rushed down the hill at a terrific pace. Both the carter and the boy, who were in their proper places at the horses' heads were dashed aside and hurled to the ground in endeavouring to stop them,

This small cross marks the spot where Alfred Watts was killed.

and unfortunately the wheels of the heavy waggon which was laden with coal . . . went over the boy's body. The boy was picked up in a senseless condition, and it was found there was no hope for the poor lad, every rib and bone in his body being fractured, and the interior parts crushed, and he expired the same evening, two hours after the occurrence.

The two little villages concerned—Mildenhall where the accident happened, and Axford a couple of miles further on where the boy lived—rang with the tragic death of 14-year-old Alfred Henry Watts, and a small memorial cross was erected in a niche in the bank of the cutting exactly opposite the spot where the lad died. But there were soon other infant deaths to share the glory and the tears, and as those most concerned died, married or moved away, memories faded. Newcomers to the villages heard the story indirectly, incompletely and sometimes inaccurately when they queried the little stone set in the bank of the hill; eventually, despite occasional clearings, the memorial itself almost vanished beneath nettles and brambles.

In October 1956 Mr Frederick Moss was driving home with three friends, all in their 60s, at about 10.30pm after visiting the cinema in Marlborough. As the car headlights swept into the cutting at Rectory Hill they lit up clearly a tall, thin, clean-shaven man standing in the middle of the road immediately opposite where all four knew the memorial stone was hidden. The man wore a long brown coat or mackintosh; his hair was grey and he stared intently to the south, his back to the cross. Although he must have been aware of the headlights, he made no attempt to move. At a distance of about 50 yards Mr Moss blew the horn, but as the figure still did not move to the side nor even turn its head, the car was forced to stop about a dozen yards away. For a few moments all four occupants stared, surprised to find a stranger, apparently drunk, in such a remote place. Mr Moss then opened the door of the car to investigate and for an instant took his eyes from the figure: immediately there was a cry of, 'He's gone.' The passengers afterwards said that it did not fade, nor did it seem to vanish—it was just that one moment it was there, the next it was not.

Although they knew that no human being could have escaped from the cutting without flying, they all got out and searched the banks on both sides with torches. Then having found no trace they sat in the darkened car for a further ten minutes hoping, yet perhaps fearing, the phantom would reappear. But the darkness remained silent, unbroken and deserted, and at length they drove the few miles home. Mr Moss's wife, a native of the village, was initially sceptical, but as the descrip-

'Although he must have been aware of the headlights he made no attempt to move.'

tion was confirmed by the other witnesses her disbelief became incredulity. Although she had been born twenty years after the accident she remembered clearly the boy's father, Henry Pounds Watts, a very tall, gaunt man, remarkable in high Edwardian England for having no whiskers or beard, and who characteristically dressed in white corduroy trousers and a long brown coat. He had died about 1907.

Why the lad's father, if indeed it was he, should have appeared to four strangers is a mystery. There was no specific anniversary—the accident had occurred in May. The only fact that may be relevant—if it is not stretching coincidence too far—is that the county council had just drawn up plans for road-widening alterations in the bank which would obliterate the niche. When these were carried out a few months later the cross was dug up and thrown with other rubble at the top of the cutting. It was over a year later that descendants of the family passing through the village noticed the absence and had the memorial replaced a few yards from its original position, where it still stands.

Mr F Moss, Polegate, Sussex

The Headless Cyclist

The winter of 1940 was a bitter one indeed for Britain: she had been pitched into a war which she seemed to be on the brink of losing; she was gripped in the claw of hard frost, and blanketed with deep snow—all events for which she was quite unprepared. But gloomy news, savage weather or the unrelieved night of the blackout was not going to stand in the way of George Dobbs when he had made up his mind to visit the local pub. In fact, terrible conditions outside were in one way an advantage in those times of shortage, as they filtered out the weaklings and the casuals leaving more room, ale and fire for the faithful.

Mr Dobbs, who had recently moved from Stafford to the outskirts of Northampton, trudged heavily towards the White Hills Hotel, where he paid a brief call to give him strength to go on to his real destination, the Fox and Hounds some half a mile further on. As he ploughed through the snow on the slope that led up past the cemetery gates he noticed a car—a relative rarity at night in petrol-starved Britain—lumbering towards him at about 15mph, its wheels following blindly the deep frozen ruts in the snow. He glanced up, and suddenly saw black against the dim headlights, a cyclist coming towards him and

'Against the headlights of the car he saw a cyclist – he seemed to be headless.'

laboriously struggling to keep his balance as he moved forward even more a prisoner of the deep gully in the snow than the car.

As George turned back to his own problems of getting through the snow, wondering whether anything was worth going out for on such a night, he realised that rather foolishly he had thought that the cyclist was headless. It had, of course, been a trick of the sharp cutoff of the headlights, or more probably because the man had very sensibly completely wrapped his head in a dark muffler against the cold. After a few moments it dawned on George, whose mind was still preoccupied with his own painful progress, that the car was not slowing down as it must do if it was to avoid an accident. He looked up again to see exactly what was happening, heard the engine growling on in low gear unchanged, and saw with horror that the vehicle was almost upon the unfortunate cyclist, who fighting desperately to keep his machine upright, seemed quite oblivious of the car immediately behind him.

Then almost before George had time to collect his thoughts the car was level with him: without stopping, without even a moment's alteration of pace, it crawled past, stumbling through the snow towards Market Harborough. There had been no sound apart from the tormented engine and the crunching of the frozen snow, but, George thought as he raced to the spot where the collision must have taken place, the snow could easily have muffled the noise of the impact. He reached the place where he had last seen the cyclist, and crossed and recrossed the road: he searched the verges in case the victim had jumped or had been thrown to one side. But there was nothing: no tangled and wrecked cycle, no mangled and broken human body. Thoroughly unnerved, George Dobbs fled as fast as the going would allow him to the Fox and Hounds at Kingsthorpe.

But despite the inner and outer warmth there, and the comforting presence of human company, he was too agitated to stay long: on the one hand there was the niggling fear that there might be a man out there lying injured in the snow, but on the other hand the greater fear that there was no man, no bicycle. He retraced his steps to the scene again and combed the area, back and forth until at last he was convinced of what he had tried not to believe. Back home his wife greeted him, ironically enough, with 'Whatever has happened to you—you look as though you had seen a ghost', and when she heard the story she was inclined to laugh the whole thing off. But George's faith in his own eyes was unshaken.

About two years later George was in the bar at the Fox and Hounds: an article on ghosts in the abbreviated sheet that passed in wartime for a newspaper had turned the conversation to the supernatural. The general opinion was one of ribald scepticism and it was with diffidence that George mentioned his experience. But it made little impression on his audience—until one of the oldest customers, Mr 'Lid' Green, for many years the local gravedigger, said as if it had been the most natural thing in the world, 'That was old ———, I buried him about 25 years ago. There was a deep snow at the time, and he was knocked off his bike just by the cemetery gates. In the crash his head was torn off his body.'

W G Dobbs, Northampton

The Kindly Ghost of Cambridge

The phantom which appears at Weston Colville Hall in West Wratting seems to be unique in its peculiarity. Weston Colville Hall, built in 1725 as a country mansion for a wealthy gentleman farmer is now divided into several separate units. At the moment two of these are gracious homes and the third the administrative offices of the D'Abo estates. Before Andrew Dodkin, his wife Marion and their baby daughter moved into their part of the mansion in May 1973 it had to be thoroughly redecorated, and to this end a working party of relatives and friends busied themselves with brushes, paste and paint in the evenings.

About 7pm one evening in mid-May Andy Dodkin's mother and father who lived nearby were busy papering an upstairs room, but found their activities severely disrupted by their Jack Russell puppy who found the vulnerable open tins of paint and pasted wallpaper delightful playthings. When he was put out in their car which was parked by the kitchen window he voiced his displeasure by howling dismally, and partly out of pity, partly out of a fear of what might happen to the interior of the car, Mr and Mrs Dodkin senior decided to take the dog home.

As Mrs Dodkin swung round the newel post at the foot of the stairs, closely followed by her husband, she saw an elderly woman hurry to the kitchen window, peer out, and then obviously reassured that there was nothing seriously wrong with the dog, turn to go back. As she did so she looked straight along the hall to face Mrs Dodkin, who saw a stranger with greying reddish hair and a high complexion, dressed in a sharply waisted long black dress with a white collar and long sleeves. The woman frowned like a child caught in some activity that had been forbidden, then hurried out of view the way she had come.

Although the figure had seemed so humanly solid and natural, Mrs Dodkin was half prepared to find the kitchen empty when she dashed in: for one thing she knew that there was no one else in that part of the house, much less a complete stranger dressed so eccentrically, but

more because, as she says 'there were straight lines down both sides of the figure as if I were watching her through a gap in a vertically boarded fence—a gap that moved about with her as she went to and fro.'

What was probably the same phantom was seen twice subsequently. On the first occasion in 1975 an agricultural student returned late one evening to pick up her car from Weston Colville Hall and seeing a light in the kitchen assumed that Marion Dodkin was there. As was usual, she went towards the house for a cup of coffee and a chat, and as she passed the window noticed casually that Marion was working at the table. When the student reached the kitchen however, it was empty as was the whole house.

One evening in the winter of 1976 Andy Dodkin had been delayed on his return from work by deep snow drifts, and unable to find a telephone box to call Marion, he was a little worried. When he eventually reached Weston Colville Hall he was not surprised to find that his wife was anxious too, and was standing in the window of the spare room he used as an office staring along the road, and well lit by light streaming in through the open door. He hurried indoors only to find that Marion was deeply asleep in bed and had obviously been so for some time. The office, and the rest of the house, when he checked, was deserted.

The Dodkins have no qualms about sharing their home with a phantom, who to judge by its concern for them and their pets, is a kindly figure. Their dog too shows none of the unease that is so common when they sense a presence. Although the house for over two and a half centuries has had a steady stream of personalities, ladies, gentlemen, men and women, passing through it, it seems that the haunt is very recent. Mrs Dodkin senior's description was immediately recognised by several older villagers to whom she mentioned her experience as a Mrs Savage—or perhaps her sister Mrs Wilby—who always dressed in that fashion, and who lived in the hall until after World War II.

Mr A Dodkin, Cambridge and Mrs R Dodkin, Cambridge

The Bleeding House

Many buildings claim to be the most haunted in Britain—almost all of them the great castles and mansions of ancient and noble families—but rather disappointingly most of them base their claim to fame on the sheer number of apparitions rather than on their diversity. Many of the phantoms, too, are very predictably said to be ancestors who have been imprisoned, murdered, separated from lovers or otherwise suffered violent fates. A more modest manor house in Sussex, mentioned in Domesday and with the fabric dating from the sixteenth century has, on the strength of the bizarre, varied and apparently unconnected phenomena that have been seen there in the last twenty years a much stronger claim.

Set in a strange hollow carved by some whim of geology in the north-facing slopes of the South Downs a few miles from Brighton, the tiny hamlet is a world apart. Its unusual geography gives it a climate markedly different from the countryside about it, and in an area where the winds make woodland sparse, it is heavily timbered—almost, indeed, overshadowed. Reached by a narrow winding lane it is a perfect setting for the supernatural, but the present owners—a pilot for a major international airline and his wife—are the last people to conjure up experiences however much their home might predispose them to do so.

The first overt demonstration that strange forces were at play in the house came in 1961 when Mrs Forster and her four children sitting at breakfast suddenly heard the unmistakable sound of a piano being played in a room immediately above them. Although the tune was unidentifiable—Mrs Forster says that it was more like improvisation—there was no doubt that it was a piano. As there was no piano of any sort in the house, the family were astounded—except the youngest son, then aged six, who said that he had heard it several times upstairs. Nothing was found, of course, but the ghostly music repeated itself some months later, since when it has remained obstinately silent.

A more disturbing incident occurred in 1963 when Mrs Forster was ironing her daughter's school blouse in the kitchen. Suddenly a gout of thick red liquid, apparently blood, dropped on the white sleeve. Mrs Forster thought at first that she must have a nose bleed, but realised that this was not the case. And when she tried immediately to remove the stain with cold water it remained indelible: nothing that was subsequently tried had any effect on the mark. When Mrs Forster returned to the ironing board she found another globule had fallen on the cover while she had been away. The ceiling, which was a modern plastered one, was unmarked, and there was no hint of a crack through which anything might have seeped. Like the music, the blood manifested itself once more—in September 1976 when Mrs Forster on returning to the kitchen she knew had been empty, found a small still-wet pool of blood on a melamine-surfaced table which had been standing in a completely different part of the room from the ironing table.

One evening in the autumn of 1973 Mrs Forster, as her husband was away, had supper with the children in her daughter's bedroom and went to bed herself early to read. A few minutes after she had got in the beautiful four-poster she heard the door open with its usual click of the latch and creak of the hinges, and assuming one of the children wanted something, she glanced up casually. To her utter amazement she saw that an elderly lady whom she did not know had entered, and now closing the door, stood with her back to it looking intently at the bed. The woman remained silent and solid as Mrs Forster, staring in astonishment, took in every detail—the grey hair, slighty waved and drawn back into a neat bun; the spectacles; the long, grey dress in time-less classic style with a low neckline and a lace jabot at the throat.

The woman paused for a few moments, and then leaning forwards slightly with her hands clasped in front of her, she advanced with quick, light, short steps. Completely bewildered, but not really afraid, Mrs Forster called out, 'Who are you? What do you want?'. Then, as if alarmed by the voice, the figure vanished: for the first time Mrs Forster realised that the elderly woman had been an apparition and not a stranger who had somehow entered the house.

A search revealed nothing, but the detailed description of the figure was instantly recognised by older inhabitants of the hamlet as that of the previous owner, a Miss Thynne, who had died tragically in a fire about fifteen years earlier. It was established that the room in which the figure appeared was the one used by Miss Thynne for many years.

Twelve months later, in the autumn of 1974, a young man from the Argentine who was visiting the family and who knew nothing of the house or of its history, slept in the same room, and rather hesitantly asked at breakfast who had been calling under the window during the night, 'Miss Thynne, Miss Thynne . . . '

Perhaps the most frightening experience at the manor occurred in 1971 in the bedroom next to the one in which the elderly lady was to appear. A family friend, an experienced hospital nurse, woke suddenly to experience first a sensation of intense suffocating heat, and then an inexplicable prickling of the scalp. Now fully awake, she saw to her terror, a pair of disembodied hands and arms floating at the normal height at the far side of the room. Before the real significance of the alarming visitation had dawned the hands began to move towards the bed in a most menacing way, and at the same time the whole atmosphere was permeated with a sense of evil. The nurse was so paralysed with dread that she could not move or cry out for help.

Gauntly silhouetted against the lighter darkness of the room, the hands with fingers extended but slightly curved, reached the posts of the bed just as she managed to begin reciting the Lord's Prayer. Whether she did it aloud or mentally she is not sure, but whichever it was the 'Deliver us from evil' had its effect and the threatening hands vanished.

At breakfast the woman was obviously very shaken indeed. She refused to spend another night in the house and although still a regular visitor, she has always since slept at a hotel a few miles away.

Name supplied, Sussex

The Eccentric Ghost of Hankham

At 12.30am on the night of 9 November 1976, 20-year-old Sophie Glessing was driving across the desolate marshes between Rye, where she had been staying for the previous seven weeks, and her home in the village of Hankham. It was one of those terrible nights that seem peculiar to this stretch of the coastline: a storm swept unimpeded from the sea across the unbroken Pevensey flats, with the sheeting rain making almost horizontal silver bars in the headlights across the black opacity of the night.

She turned off the A279 coastal road between its filling dykes to the unclassified lane leading to Jenkins Green and Hankham, relieved that she was only a couple of miles from her bed. As she reached the crest of Mill Hill her headlamps lit up the bizarre figure of a well-known local character, a Mr Hawkley, trudging along in the teeth of the storm towards his cottage at the top of the rise. While a stranger would have been extremely startled at the sight of an elderly balding man with a full blond beard, dressed only in green and pink pyjamas, a camel dressing-gown and slippers shuffling along the middle of a country road in such appalling weather late at night, he was familiar enough to Sophie. Since the death of his wife a few years earlier Mr Hawkley had become a little odd in his behaviour, one of his more widely reported eccentricities being his nocturnal excursions in his nightwear.

Sophie slowed down to offer the old man a lift, but as her car came almost to a halt she realised that his cottage was not more than 20 yards ahead and that in the time it took him to ease his stiffening limbs into her low sports car he could be in the shelter and warmth of his home. Accordingly, she waved cheerily and accelerated on her way. The following morning at breakfast she commented casually to her mother that the old man was still taking his strange rambles. Mrs Glessing turned sharply, while Sophie explained how she had almost offered him a lift in the storm during the night. 'But', said Mrs Glessing, 'you could not have seen Mr Hawkley—he died three weeks ago.'

Sophie Glessing, Eastbourne

Historical Hauntings

The Faithful Friar

Crouching low and ancient in the Hampshire downs the tiny village of Buriton has an air of timeless tranquility. Moist winds sweeping in from the sea fill the hollow with a gentle white mist, appropriate enough a setting for three ghosts which have been seen there in recent years—one of them reported from three different locations by three separate sets of witnesses. The heart of the village is a large pond, on one side of which is the church and rectory, and on the other the large sprawling manor house which like so many in the region has been added to so often over the centuries that it is a living lesson in architecture. It is in this manor house that two of the Buriton ghosts are regularly seen—so regularly, in fact, that in 1957 the then occupier, Colonel Bonham Carter, made their presence a reason for an application for a reduction in rates. Though the chairman of the tribunal wondered whether an established haunting might not be an added amenity and so be grounds for an increase, the reduction was granted.

On a number of occasions children at the manor have seen an elderly, smiling woman indulgently watching them at play, and from their descriptions it seems that she was a nursemaid of the period of the Gibbons (*Decline and Fall*) family who occupied the manor for much of the eighteenth century and who built the Georgian wing in which this ghost is invariably seen.

More spectacular and more frequent is the maid who is seen to hurry from the Tudor part of the house of the manor, across the wide courtyard and through a high brick wall towards the church. A careful examination of the footing and the brickwork shows that at the spot where the girl melts there was once a gateway, filled in probably in the nineteenth century. Although the lady's haste may be an excess of piety, there are, as always, rumours of a rape or murder, but nothing is known which could account for this persistence of either of the manor servants.

Perhaps the most important ghost of Buriton is that of the friar who has been seen by at least four people in recent years. In the 1960s 11-year-old Jamie, who was living at the manor and who was a keen horseman, brought his pony into the stable yard at dusk one Sunday afternoon and was startled by a man whom he described as looking like a monk in a brown cloak standing silently behind a bale of straw. It did not enter his head that the figure was anything other than a real person, and his fear was not of the supernatural but of a rather menacing human

Buriton Manor.

stranger loitering in the yard. He said nothing indoors but made an entry in his diary: his parents did notice however that he was silent and withdrawn all the evening and showed an unusual reluctance to go to the stable the following day. On Tuesday his mother noticed the diary and contacted the rector, who talked for a long time with the boy and who went with him to the spot in the yard. Jamie described in detail the brown habit, the white cord knotted round the waist, but could give no information about the feet because these had been hidden behind the bale.

What the boy told him convinced the rector that the figure was not of a monk but of a friar—Buriton never had any monastic institution, and although the manor had been owned by the Benedictines before the Reformation it had always been let to a tenant lay farmer. As the story of Jamie's apparition became known in the village the rector was approached by a churchwarden who told him that the previous year she and her daughter had been gathering wild roses near the spot where a narrow lane from the village crosses the busy A3 road when they saw a man 'like a monk' in a brown cloak with a white cord with tassels on the ends. They both assumed that it was someone playing a trick or trying to frighten them, and walked towards the figure which was a hundred yards or so away to see who it was. As they neared, it vanished on completely open ground.

These reports led the rector to look again at accounts left by one of his predecessors who had been the incumbent from 1936–1952. The canon had been working in the rectory garden when he noticed a brown-robed figure approaching along an avenue of beech trees behind the house, significantly known as Monks' Walk. He put down his fork to see what the stranger wanted and immediately the figure vanished. The canon could not believe a supernatural explanation and asked the maid indoors who had called: he was told that no one as far as she knew had been near the house. The canon's wife reported too that she had on several occasions in the garden heard footsteps from the area of the Monks' Walk, and on one afternoon they were so clear that she assumed that it was her husband returning and went into the house to put the kettle on for tea.

Perhaps one of the most interesting facts is that the friar has been seen in three different places in a space of two miles along the line of the ancient ridge trackway that leads from Buriton to East Meon and so on to Winchester. On this track too, some distance beyond the sighting by the churchwarden is a remote stile which is marked on some maps as Friar's Knapp. Unlike monks, who remained inside the monastery grounds, friars wandered from village to village on regular circuits like judges, finding hospitality where they could or else sleeping hungry under a hedge. Perhaps one brother, quite understandably, fell so much in love with the beauty of his round that he has been ambling gently along the crest of the downs and into the valleys for over four centuries.

Rev Peter Gallup, Winchester

The Wandering Puritan

In January 1974 22-year-old Geoffrey, together with Francis Ponder of Tolleshunt d'Arcy and two other young men, travelled towards Manchester to watch their local first division football team, Ipswich, play Manchester United. About 11am they stopped at the Keele Service Area on the M6 motorway, where Geoffrey and Francis went to the toilet leaving their companions in the car. There were only a few people in the cloakroom at the time, most of them unremarkable. But the man standing at the urinal between Geoffrey and Francis riveted their attention even though no one else seemed to notice his eccentricity. 'He was', says Geoffrey, 'like one of those pictures you see of Puritans. He had a wide-brimmed hat, a broad white collar and buff-coloured clothes. I noticed particularly the very coarse stitching and the fact that the material seemed well-worn and shabby.'

When the man left Geoffrey and Francis wondered who he could be and assumed that he must be connected with a film or advertising stunt. Mildly intrigued they hurried out after him only to find that there was no trace of him. They asked their friends in the car, but they were positive that no such person had come through the door. All were a little mystified because the figure had been so definite and so distinctive, and there seemed nowhere he could have gone without being noticed after he had left the cloakroom. Nevertheless, in the excitement of the day the incident was dismissed.

Some months later Geoffrey was standing at a front window in the home of his parents-in-law which faced the Siege House in Colchester, a bullet-pitted building which was the last stronghold of the Royalist forces before they surrendered to the Parliamentary troops in the Civil War. He suddenly gave an excited shout. The figure he had seen in the Keele Service Area was walking slowly along the pavement opposite. Again, as in the toilet, no one seemed to notice him, and though he did not appear to take any deliberate avoiding action he never seemed to get in anyone's way or to bump into anyone.

Geoffrey's frantic yell brought his wife and mother-in-law running in from the back of the house: side by side they stood staring into the roadway as he pointed out the figure which by now had been in uninterrupted vision for some 25 yards. Christine, his wife, looked blankly and asked what was the matter as all she could see were ordinary people passing to and fro, but his mother-in-law, absolutely astounded, described in detail the figure that he had seen over a hundred miles away. After a few more seconds it passed out of the field of view, vanishing as a normal human being would have done because it was hidden by the window frame.

Geoffrey thinks that he saw the figure again, this time in some fields near Colchester, but has asked for it not to be considered as a completely objective sighting, firstly because he was alone at the time and had no one to corroborate his statement, and secondly, because of the two previous experiences very much on his mind he may have projected the apparition quite unconsciously. Geoffrey has little interest in history, and none in this rather specialised period: 'If I had been going to imagine something from the past,' he says, 'I would have found a person much more interesting than this one.'

Geoffrey Wright, Colchester

'He was like one of those pictures you see of Puritans.'

The Monk on the Wall

Penwortham Secondary School is one of those ubiquitous raw-brick-and-glass buildings that mushroomed in the 1950s and 1960s to provide the new education that would enable the new generation to cope with the technology and leisure that their parents in the bad old days had never dreamed of. But despite the revolution in accommodation and academic method, little had changed basically, and so it was in the winter of 1968 14-year-old Valerie Sandham was sitting passively in classroom C11, a rarely used room at the end of one of those endless corridors. The lesson was religious knowledge, a subject which did not hold her enthralled but at which she worked hard because she invari-

Penwortham Secondary School.
Valerie Sandham.

ably did well in examinations on it: there was little apart from the teaching to distract her attention—three blank, cream-painted walls without windows to her front, rear and right, and on her left an expanse of glass which gave a view across the playing fields that after four years was so familiar that even the blackboard was a more interesting prospect.

Halfway through the lesson Valerie's attention was suddenly caught by a vague movement to the right of the teacher, between the blackboard and the door. She turned slightly to look more closely, and was dumbfounded to see what appeared to be the profile of a monk—or at least, a hooded man—seated at a writing desk. There was no question from the start that it was real because the apparition was a two-dimensional white shadow, seemingly imprinted on the cream wall about two feet from the floor. 'Try to imagine,' says Valerie, 'a life-size moving cardboard cutout, mistily filled in . . .' and with that strange quirk in human observation that tends to fasten on completely irrelevant details, she remembers vividly the long nose of the elderly man, and the quill which from time to time he dipped in an inkwell at the side of the desk.

For some moments she sat staring with incredulity, and then with the practicality that is supposed to be traditional in Lancashire, she began to doubt her own senses and to look for a logical situation. She checked that the light from the window was not causing a shadow from the teacher, but in any case the figure was lighter, not darker than the wall, and had a life and movement quite independent of the master taking the lesson. Having exhausted all natural possibilities, she was forced back to her original and spontaneous explanation—the supernatural—and nudged her companion to look. But as her friend turned, rather cautiously as they were in the front desk immediately beneath the teacher's eye, the apparition faded.

Valerie was bursting with the story when she arrived home but her mother, who had had a very strange experience in Lancaster some years earlier, was well aware how people treated such reports and advised her not to mention it to anyone. Valerie said nothing, but although she looked intently every time she went into the classroom again, she saw nothing. Nevertheless, every detail remained very clear in her mind.

Four years later Valerie was working as a dental nurse in Preston, and was joined at the surgery by another girl, Hazel Coulton, from Penwortham. Discussing school-days in a nostalgic way, Hazel one day mentioned a strange apparition she had seen one afternoon on the wall of classroom C11: as she listened, without saying a word, Valerie heard her own story in precise detail, even to the desk in which she had been sitting. Neither girl could remember the slightest reference to monasticism in any previous lesson, and tried to relate the apparition to the place. It was not a profitable line: the site of the school, as far as they

'The figure of a monk was like a life-size cardboard cutout. He had a very large nose and held a quill.'

could discover, had never been anything but farmland, though the ruins of an old farmhouse were very close to the wing which terminated in the haunted classroom.

Mrs N Sandham and Mrs Valerie Spink, Lancashire

Rider from the Past

The bitterness of the English Civil War has left traditions and hauntings scattered up and down the country with the corpses. Shropshire, which was relatively lightly touched by pitched battles, has no such ghostly spectacles as the phantom armies which were locked night after night in conflict at Edgehill, but what it lacks in magnificence it makes up for in style. One of the most enduring legends of the region from Cromwellian times is that of the escape of Major Smalman.

The major, a dogmatic and irascible lordling in true medieval fashion, was a fanatical royalist, and after he had killed his relative Edward Kinnersley in combat in Mogg Forest because he happened to support the parliamentary cause, he became an obvious target for Roundhead troops mopping up pockets of resistance as the King's power collapsed. In about 1645 Major Smalman's home, Wilderthorpe Hall, now a National Trust property, was surrounded by a troop of parliament's horsemen, but in the confusion the major managed to slip past them. He was, however, soon spotted galloping north-east along the wild country of Wenlock Edge, and was immediately pursued.

On reaching what is now Blakeway Coppice, to the amazement of his attackers, he suddenly swung his horse to the left and leapt over the edge of the escarpment which at this point plunges a precipitous 30 yards. Whether there was any pressing tactical reason for such a suicidal move is not known, but if it did occur it can hardly have been accidental, for Major Smalman must have known every inch of the countryside from a lifetime of hunting over it. According to the story, the parliamentary troops were convinced that such a fall must be fatal, and abandoned the chase to return to the more leisurely and more profitable occupation of looting the major's home. But Smalman, by luck or skill, managed to end up—bruised, dishevelled but still very much alive—in a crab apple tree, while his horse crashed to its death below.

Strangely enough there has never been any suggestion that a ghostly horseman gallops along the Edge and leaps in true Western style into the void over the precipice—only the tradition, and the words 'Major's Leap' remain. The name appears near the hamlet of Stretton Westwood, but the site is a matter of dispute and local historians and students find evidence to place it in half a dozen widely-separated spots along Wenlock Edge. But they are working from vague sources recorded many years after the actual event: the strange story of Eva and Alick Knight throws a completely new light on the whole episode of Major Smalman's flight and his dramatic leap.

Until 1967 the Knights were both lecturers in Art colleges in London, and as Alick's retirement approached they bought a remote and semi-derelict farmhouse at Chatwall in Shropshire. In the two years prior to giving up full-time work they travelled from London to Shropshire every holiday, repairing, renovating and decorating: neither of them knew anything of the county apart from the main road to Church Stretton, and from then onwards, the narrow winding lane to Chatwall. Alick was a Sussex man, and Eva had come from Germany as a teenage refugee in 1938, so that neither of them had the remotest idea of the Smalman legend.

At Easter 1965 the Knights passed through the little settlement of Enchmarsh about 3.30 on a bright, sunny April afternoon, on the last couple of miles to their future home along a single lane track. For about half the distance the road climbs steadily, and then drops to the hollow where Chatwall Hall and Home Farm squat in some shelter from the sweeping winds. As they approached the top of the rise, travelling very slowly to revel in the Marcher countryside in the soft settling light of the late afternoon sun, they were suddenly delighted by the appearance of a large black horse standing sideways in the middle of the track just ahead of them. The rider, whose wide-brimmed, large-plumed hat, cloak and breeches were characteristic of a mid-seventeenth-century nobleman, seemed not to have noticed their approach, and sitting motionless on his horse with his clothes moving in the hilltop breeze, stared steadily to the west.

Mrs Knight slowed the car almost to a halt, as both she and her husband watched, silent and fascinated by the unexpected pleasure. Then, still without any hint that they were conscious of the car, horse and rider leaped into the field on the left-hand side of the track, turned sharply, and then galloped southwards parallel to the roadway. The Knights followed their progress as long as they were visible, and then, starting up again, drove the remaining mile to their house. Only when they were inside did they speak again: Eva asked her husband if he had noticed anything unusual along the lane, and Alick described in detail with the eye of an artist exactly what she had seen—with one small difference. Mr Knight interpreted the rider's disappearance with the mental vision of reason, and said that he had gone over the brow of the hill: Mrs Knight was adamant that he had vanished when all the laws of optics said that he should still be in sight.

On further discussion they both agreed that strangely enough horse and rider had appeared in monochrome—greys and blacks—with only the feather standing out a clear, vivid white, and that despite the fact that the car window was open, they had heard no sound as the pair had 'thundered' past only a few yards away. Still there was no suggestion of the supernatural: the only explanation seemed to be that an historical film was being made in the neighbourhood, or that someone was practising for a pageant, but enquiries the following morning drew a complete blank on both these activities. No one could identify either the horse or its rider from the Knights' description, and it was only when these lines of enquiry had been exhausted that they were reluctantly forced to consider the possibility of ghosts.

When Eva began to investigate, still no one mentioned the Smalman affair, perhaps because there was never any suggestion that he had appeared in phantom form, and in any case 'his' site was at least nine miles to the east. But when looked at on the ground, the possibility that the Knights' apparition was Major Smalman grows: Chatwall is certainly nearer Wilderthorpe Hall than Stretton Westwood and over much easier terrain. It seems probable too that under the circumstances a fugitive might well have preferred to make north-west towards the wild country of the Long Myndd, and the even wilder country of Wales for a hiding place, rather than north-east which would bring him back into parliamentary territory.

To their disappointment, although they have passed the spot hundreds of times since that April afternoon in 1965, Eva and Alick Knight have never caught another glimpse of their apparition: perhaps the major—if it was he—was not on this occasion on his desperate flight, but merely with feudal proprietorship, inspecting new arrivals in his area.

Eva Knight, Church Stretton, Shropshire

Sympathetic Shadows

The phantoms of Sherrington Manor are in the grand old classical tradition and setting. The manor has a continuous documented history since the Domesday Book, and even when this was compiled in the eleventh century the site is almost certain to have been occupied for many hundreds of years. For over 900 years the owners have been prosperous

farming squires, living busy but quiet lives, and meriting named tombs in the churchyard and the word 'gentleman' in their epitaphs.

The present building dates from the late middle ages, and like so many ancient houses it had been added to and altered so much over the centuries that when it was bought by the present owners, the Chandless family, in 1873 it was a haphazard maze of rooms, corridors and staircases. In the 1870s the interior was rationalised—seven stairways that ran from the ground floor to the bedrooms, for example, were reduced to two.

Although the alterations do not seem to have provoked any presences to make themselves visible, either in approval or annoyance, the family accepted almost as part of everyday living strange noises from various parts of the house. The long gallery on the first floor is a particularly strong focus of activity, and over the years right up to the present day scores of people have heard the heavy footsteps of a man passing to and fro above their heads when it was known there was no one upstairs. Though the ancient boards creak when the smallest child walks over them, the now familiar measured tread does not raise the faintest squeak. At other times people in the gallery have been conscious of the quiet rustle and swish of what appears to be silk clothing brushing past them towards a bedroom door at the end where loud, imperious knocks are heard before a death or major disaster in the immediate family. On other occasions footsteps have been heard apparently moving diagonally from the floor of the hall upwards towards the gallery; then it was realised that the sounds seemed to be following the line of one of the staircases removed during the nineteenth-century alterations.

In May 1957 the first known visible manifestation occurred, and though it seems probable, it is not possible to say definitely whether or not this is related to the male footsteps. Seven adults—Mr and Mrs Chandless, their three grown-up children and two friends—were sitting talking after lunch when a man dressed in a coarsely woven brown garment variously described as a cloak or duffel-coat walked across the hall past the open dining room door towards the kitchen entrance. Four of the people present—that is, those who could actually see the hall from where they sat—immediately questioned who he could be: it was broad daylight, and the man's purposeful step seemed to indicate that he knew where he was going. No one had the faintest idea that he was anything other than a normal human being who had entered without ringing and was looking for someone. Mrs Chandless went casually to make enquiries, but when after finding no one about the

'She knew from their voices and the sound of their footsteps that they were a woman and a small child. The woman said, "Sssh . . . . she's asleep I think".'

house, and knowing there was no way in which he could have left without being seen, she roused the others to search. Nothing was found, and when after a while it was realised that the figure must have been an apparition, it was not the fact that a ghost had appeared that surprised those who had seen it, but that the whole thing was so prosaically ordinary. It was only later when the transition from the familiar audible manifestation to the visual one was being talked about was it realised that none of the four witnesses had noticed the figure's face: all commented that their attention had been drawn to the texture of the material of the cloak.

Perhaps the most touching of the phenomena that have occurred at Sherrington took place in 1955, and again, may be connected with the rustlings in the long gallery. Therese, an Austrian au-pair-companion who had been in the house for a few months had frequently mentioned that she could not keep her bedroom door closed no matter how carefully she fastened it or how often workmen were called in to check the lock. She probably attributed its peculiar behaviour to nothing more abnormal than the age of the house and the inadequacies of British workmen—until, that is, one afternoon when she was resting on her bed with a mild migraine.

Suddenly, she says, she found herself incapable of moving, though she was wide awake and her senses were acute. Her back was to the door, when she heard it open quietly and two people entered the room. Though she could not turn round she knew from their voices and the sound of their footsteps that they were a woman and a small child. The pair tiptoed to the bedside and peered down: then the woman's voice said quite clearly, 'Sssh . . . she's asleep I think.' The two people turned, moved gently across the room and closed the door: immediately Therese found that she could move and jumping from bed she rushed out into the long gallery after the visitors who had only a few seconds start. But the gallery and the stairs were empty: downstairs she was told that no one had been near the house that afternoon.

Although no one at Sherrington was clearly aware of the facts until they were pointed out by an historian working on local documents some 20 years after Therese's experience, in 1819 the new, young mistress of the manor, 26-year-old Mary Skinner, died suddenly only a fortnight after the death of her five-year-old daughter Katherine. Whether the same infection carried off them both, or whether Mary died of grief after the loss of her daughter is not known, but it would be interesting to know whether the room in which the sympathetic shadows appeared was the one in which either or both of the Skinners

The long gallery, Sherrington Manor.
Hallway of the Manor where the ghost in the brown coat was seen.

had died so tragically over a century and a half earlier. If the apparitions were of Mary and Katherine, one wonders too what brought them back—was it profound pity for some other woman who was lonely, lost and ill?

Mrs Chandless, Sussex

The Spectral Army

The most frequently reported of all hauntings are certainly ghostly footsteps, and while many of these are undoubtedly genuine, there are also many explanations for this type of sound. Creaking or contracting woodwork or brick; loose structures flapping in a wind; a bough tapping against a wall—all give a very realistic imitation of a heavy walk. The rhythmic beat of a body of men marching, however, is much less likely to be confused with any other natural sound especially if it is heard out of doors. Yet from a number of places in Britain—Edgehill in Warwickshire, Keswick in Cumbria and Echt in Aberdeenshire to name only the best known—the sound of tramping armies has been reported.

The most famous story is from Edgehill where in 1643, a year after the first major battle of the Civil War, disturbing rumours reached Charles I. A royal commission of three officers under Colonel Lewis Kirke and 'three gentlemen of credit' was sent to the spot to investigate: after taking sworn depositions from a number of local people, including the magistrate and the minister, they themselves watched on the site of the battle and according to a pamphlet published early in 1643, they saw and heard on two separate occasions a complete re-enactment of the fight, even to recognising many of their comrades who had died there. Apparitions on such a vast scale and appearing to so many people are, of course, extremely rare, and perhaps today many believe that over the centuries the story has been grossly exaggerated, but a report from two reliable witnesses in 1951 suggests that the old accounts may have a strong element of truth in them.

In July 1951 Joyce Nicholls, a nurse, and her friend, Frances Robinson, an accountant, were holidaying in Dunster in Somerset. From their headquarters in the fourteenth-century Luttrell Arms Hotel they explored the general tourist run of the town and castle, and after a few days began to wander further afield. In the course of their walks they reached Conygar Hill, some miles to the north. This very steeply-rising tor, whose slopes were covered with small trees and shrubs, was surmounted by a circular battlemented tower—in fact a folly built by the Luttrell family in 1760—which intrigued them so much that brushing aside their own professional respectability and the owner's 'Private Property—No Entry' notice, they scrambled under the barbed wire fence and began the ascent.

But the gradient was much sharper than they had estimated from the roadway, and it was only by hauling themselves up by branches of trees and the shrubs that they were able to reach the top, breathless and exhausted. The view from the summit however, made the effort worthwhile: above was the brittle, cloudless sky of a blazing summer's day, and thrown about their feet was the great circle of the lush Somerset countryside, dominated to the south by the grey pile of the castle. Intoxicated by the beauty, the two women slipped into the tower, and climbing the sloping ramp, reached the top.

At last satisfied, they came back down and standing outside the eerie gloom of the stone cylinder were immediately aware that a change had taken place in the atmosphere in the short time they had been inside. The sun still burned relentlessly from an unbroken sky, but a bitterly chill wind wrapped round them as if in a few moments they had been transported to winter. At the same time too, they felt a darkening of the light about them as if a cloud was passing over the brightness. Both felt a deep sense of unease, not born alone of the changed physical conditions for which there seemed no natural reason, and then both swung simultaneously round to the north from where there came the faint but unmistakable sound of a large group of people marching towards them.

They were horrified, for they both knew that even if there had been no undergrowth or trees on the slope it was far too steep for anyone to walk up at that speed, and in any case, the steps drumming in rhythm seemed to be coming along a horizontal path at their own level. In the ladies' minds there was no doubt that an invisible, phantom army was approaching, and as the beating steps came nearer and nearer, the wind seemed to increase until the trees on the hillside swayed. At the same time the gloom thickened, and then, just when what must have been the front rank of the spectral troops was almost level, the women's nerves broke. They hurled themselves almost suicidally down the hill through the bushes and brambles, heedless of the thorns that ripped their faces and arms and legs. Absolute fear held them until some minutes later they reached the foot of the hill and threw themselves, breathless and sobbing, on their stomachs under the wire fence. Only then as they stood up in the roadway with the sun baking down, and the air still and hot round them like a warm bath did they dare to look back up. The hill was folded in the heat: the trees were motionless and the air calm and silent. Of the marching feet there was not the slightest sound.

Back in their hotel and changed from their torn clothing, the two women asked the owner if he had heard of any similar experiences, but whether his non-committal reply that people usually took notice of the private property sign concealed any deeper knowledge, they never knew. Apart from some very bitter engagements in the Civil War when Dunster Castle was held by both sides in succession, no major battle seems to be known from the area, but not far to the east lies Sedgemoor with its tragic memories of the Monmouth rebellion of 1683, and to the west and further back in time, is the traditional Arthurian country. Who can say whose the marching footsteps might have been—the men of Arthur's army, Parliamentarians or Royalists, rebelling peasants, or even armies from one of the many forgotten encounters of the middle ages, when Dunster Castle was indeed a fortress.

Miss F Robinson, Brighton ·

Bronze Age Horseman

What is probably recognised as the oldest known ghost comes from Bottlebush Down in north Dorset, where a horse and rider are said to gallop beside the A3081 road which wanders from Cranborne to Sixpenny Handley. This area, now remote, must in antiquity have been a centre of activity: the important Roman road from Badbury to Salisbury crosses it. A strange earthwork called the Cursus, consisting of two parallel ditches and banks 80 yards apart, which runs for six miles, must once have been heavily garrisoned; the fields are dotted with low, round burial barrows, indicating a region well populated by the standards of 2,000 to 3,000 years ago.

Shepherds on the downs here have for long had a tradition of a spectral horseman who appears from a wood near the Roman road and gallops westwards towards the Cursus: in the late 1920s two frightened girls who had cycled at night from Handley to Cranborne reported to the police that they had been terrified by a man on horseback who had appeared suddenly and had ridden soundlessly beside them. No doubt these, and more recent though more vague, sightings would have turned the apparition into a medieval knight, a lost cavalier, a headless coachman, or more probably as this is the heart of the Judge Jeffreys country, a Monmouth supporter fleeing desperately for his life after Sedgemoor, had not the figure been observed by a trained archaeologist, Mr R C Clay.

In 1924 Mr Clay was in charge of the excavations of a Bronze Age site near Christchurch, and drove back each evening to his home near Salisbury. One night, as he was passing the spot where the line of the old Roman road crosses the A3081, he was conscious of a horseman galloping as if to cut across the highway ahead of him: when he slowed down the horse was turned and ran parallel and level with the car, some 50 yards from it.

In the traffic-free days of the mid-twenties, Mr Clay had time to observe the figure in detail: he saw the smallish horse with a long tail and mane, but without bridle or stirrups: he saw the bare legs and long flowing cloak of the rider, who appeared to be brandishing a weapon over his head. Whether this was in greeting or aggression Mr Clay did not have time to discover for after about 100 yards the apparition vanished.

As dusk was thickening Mr Clay did not stop: in any case he was probably a little uneasy, for his specialist knowledge enabled him to date the figure fairly definitely as the late Bronze Age (700–600 BC), but he did make a careful mental note of all the landmarks for investigation by daylight. On his return the following day he noted that there was a low burial mound exactly where the horseman had disappeared, but nothing else which could account for the strange rider: for weeks he tried in all lighting conditions to find bushes, or tricks of posts and parallax which could have confused him in the half light. He found nothing, and having tried every scientific means of convincing himself that he had been mistaken, he was forced to the conclusion that he had indeed witnessed the re-enactment of a ride almost 3,000 years old.

Collated from diverse sources

Poltergeists and Evil Ghosts

The Tenement of Terror

It is a popular jibe that a ghost is a good ally for council tenants who want to change their house, or for private tenants who want a reduction in rent. But when two nurses run out of an ideal flat in the early hours of the morning and refuse to sleep there again, even though they have no alternative accommodation, we must look further than mere whim or convenience for the source of their behaviour.

In the autumn of 1974 Shirley Brown came from her home in Orkney to be a student nurse at Dundee Hospital, and after about six months she was fortunate enough to find a small flat in a tenement in Morgan Street. Here she shared a livingroom-kitchen, bathroom and bedroom with fellow student Gail Bruce, and for a year life seemed idyllic. Both girls enjoyed their work and studies; got on extremely well with each other; were free to run their own lives, and for Shirley at least, a mainland city was still exciting.

Then in January 1976 something went seriously wrong: one morning Shirley who was not to be on duty until 1pm did not waken until Gail was about to leave for the morning shift, and found her flatmate looking at her with a very strange expression. Gail asked whether Shirley felt all right, and scarcely waiting for the affirmative answer, said that she would explain at lunchtime. Over the midday meal Gail said that she had been unable to sleep the night before for no obvious reason—Shirley herself had last looked at her watch at 2.30, but neither of them realised that the other was awake—when at about 3.30 as near as she could guess, the hall light suddenly snapped on. Immediately afterwards she heard someone moving about in the bathroom with slow, padding steps, and not unnaturally she was terrified, although logically she knew that as the door was locked no one could possibly get in.

Gail dived beneath the bedclothes but after a few minutes her natural curiosity got the better of her and she emerged. The hall was now in darkness again, but with a numbing sensation compounded of surprise and fear, she saw standing beside Shirley's bed what she took to be a normal, elderly woman with short grey hair and dressed in a pale blue nightgown or long dress.

The stranger and Shirley were apparently deep in conversation in sibilant whispers, and though Gail could not make out any actual words there seemed an overwhelming impression of evil and menace in the secretive muttering. Momentarily she closed her eyes, then reopened them, and found the figure gone: petrified and uncomprehending she lay tensed in the darkness until, rather prematurely, she got up for duty. Both girls were now very frightened by the incident, and decided that they would never be in the flat alone again. One evening a week later, however, just as their fears were beginning to subside and the tension to relax, Shirley was lying in bed just before midnight reading as she waited for Gail to finish in the bathroom. Gradually she became aware, to the steadily-increasing pounding of her heart, that someone was moving stealthily about the kitchen. Immediately the tide of fear flooded back, and simultaneously she thought she could hear Gail still in the bathroom. Apprehensively she tapped the wall that divided bedroom from kitchen, knowing that if Gail were in the kitchen she would tap back.

But instead of a reassuring, gentle, feminine knock, there came a terrible outburst as if someone with superhuman strength and steel talons was trying to claw a way through the brickwork. Frantically Shirley called for Gail, who dashed in from the bathroom, and at once the terrifying sounds fell to a silence that was almost as frightening. The two girls sat on the bed, struggling to hold at bay the panic that threatened to engulf them, when there came again the savage clawing at the wall, this time with increased ferocity as if the being on the other side was determined to smash through. For over a quarter of an hour the frenzied battering and tearing continued until without warning their nerves snapped, and pulling on a few clothes they prepared to dash from the building although it was now almost 1am.

The instant they were ready they realised with horror that their keys were in the livingroom, which was now occupied by something dreadful. But not wishing to stay where they were, they plucked up every atom of courage they possessed, raced into the hall and flicked on the electric light in the livingroom. There was instantly a brilliant blue flash, and the bulb fused—this may have been sheer coincidence, but the darkness did not make the perilous dash across the room to the table any less terrifying.

Very upset, they spent the rest of the night in the flat of friends, who had it not been for the very genuine state of shock the two stable and strong-minded girls were in, would have dismissed the whole affair as nonsense or hysteria. Neither of them dared spend another night in their own flat though they did go back in daylight hours to collect their belongings. They noticed that the wall, in spite of the frenzied clawing they had heard, had not the slightest mark on it. Although both felt that they should try to find out more of the history of the flat—if only for their own peace of mind—and get some idea of what might be behind the haunting, their nerves would not let them lest they turned up something more dreadful than they had anticipated. In the peace of new rooms they found a week later, they were only too glad to let the terror of those two nights fade gradually from the forefront of their minds.

Miss Shirley A Brown, Dundee

The Shapeless Evil

It is not very often that a ghost is malevolent. Frequently it is neutral, appearing erratically and apparently pointlessly as if it had some fixed psychic routine to perform whether it had an audience or not. At other times it seems to have a conscious and logical purpose for making itself known in a specific place at a specific time to a particular person. Only rarely do hauntings seem to harm deliberately, and this makes the terrifying experience of Mrs Joy McKenna at Broadway in 1971 all the more mystifying.

At the time Mrs McKenna was living in a large Cotswold stone house which, though built only in 1936, stood on ground which had had a turbulent history and which had seen much violence in early days. When her husband had to make business trips which necessitated his starting early in the morning he usually slept in one of the guest rooms to avoid waking his wife—despite the fact that she invariably set her alarm clock to coincide with his so that she could prepare his breakfast.

It was on such an occasion in November 1971 that Joy McKenna set her alarm for 6.30 when she went to bed at about 11pm, and fell asleep almost immediately. She woke some time later and as she normally anticipated the ringing of the alarm bell by some minutes, she assumed that it was already morning. Her first reaction in the half-conscious state was a reluctance to leave the cosy warmth, a mild annoyance that the night had been so short—and then, suddenly, both feelings were obliterated by a terrifying sense of apprehension. She was aware, by what senses she does not know, that something was present in the room, moving along the side of her bed: the shock of an intruder cleared the last wisps of sleep from her mind but the faint hope that it might be her husband was shattered by the sound of his gentle snoring from the next room.

The awful sense of overpowering fear swamped a lifetime of rational thought and with the blind faith of billions of children in the dark, she sought safety under the bedclothes. Instantly the form creeping

'She could see two terrible eyes, long, amber and burning with evil.'

88

stealthily about the room leaped on her with immense weight as she huddled beneath the blankets, and writhing and mauling, it began physically to pummel her shoulders, arms and chest like a demented beast. Joy McKenna was conscious of being crushed, and then to her indescribable horror found that when she tried to escape the beating every muscle had locked in paralysis: although she could still move her mouth she could not make it utter any sound.

But in the rigid catalepsy of the body her mind remained crystal clear: her thoughts spun round the sheer impossibility of the situation, how utterly irrational it all was, that this was her death. She had never thought of dying as such fearful torment. Although her brain told her rationally it was impossible because she was in complete darkness beneath the bedding, she could see clearly two terrible eyes, long, amber and burning with evil, like those of some demon in the most savage of oriental art, staring at her. At the same time she had a sensation of a fearful cacophony of noise—a screaming discordancy which she knew logically she could not hear with her ears, but which was all about her.

Then the deepest parts of her reason found the answer: she prayed vehemently, begging God to drive away the intensity of evil in the room. And immediately she was conscious of the immense weight slithering in a strange obscene fashion over the side of the bed to the floor. The moment the pressure lifted and she could move, she screamed and hurled herself from the bed to her knees to pray. A moment or two later her husband rushed in, alarmed by her shouts, and found her frantic, her face a cold, ashy grey. As they sat for the rest of the night round a fire, sipping coffee and brandy, her husband gradually became convinced that what Joy McKenna had experienced was not, as he had naturally assumed, a nightmare of particularly brutal intensity. They looked coldly at events of the recent past to try to find something that might offer a clue, but found nothing—until Mrs McKenna remembered the strange incident in the same bedroom a few days earlier.

The McKennas are fond of their four cats, who share with the family the freedom of the house. No serious objection is raised to their sleeping on the beds, nor in cold weather crawling under the covers for warmth. Two days earlier Joy had gone to the bedroom and had noticed a hump under the counterpane, which she assumed was one of her pets. After a moment, however, the shape slithered almost like a fish over the side of the bed and vanished. She was slightly surprised, first because it had disappeared without greeting her, and secondly because its movements had been so unnatural. The cats normally stood up, arched their backs and stretched, whereas on this occasion the creature had, without changing its shape, glided away with a single sinuous movement. Her puzzlement was increased when she went downstairs and found all four animals shut up in the dining room.

For the rest of their stay at the house the McKennas experienced nothing that could throw any light on the frightening events. Perhaps the entity that invaded the building was not what many people would call a ghost at all, but some utterly malevolent manifestation which has nothing to do with the human spirit—an impersonal, illogical, uncontrolled and wholly evil supernatural force.

Mrs Joy McKenna, Bristol

The Beckoning One

Mrs Gladys Ewing of Aberdeen has an even greater problem than usual in convincing people of the truth of her supernatural experience, because it took place in the early morning of New Year's Day—a time when even those normally inclined to believe might suggest a confusion between spirits of the bottled and psychic variety. Mrs Ewing spent New Year's Eve, 1970, at her daughter's home on the Kincorthland estate, but as both she and her son-in-law had to be on duty early the following morning—she at the Morningfield hospital and he at the prison—Hogmanay was a quiet family affair, with a single small whisky at midnight and bed immediately afterwards.

At a quarter to six in the morning the streets of the estate were eerily deserted, though brightly lit, as Gladys Ewing went down the path on her way to the bus stop. As she closed the garden gate she glanced casually in the direction she was going, and to her utter disbelief she saw standing about 100 yards away from her on one of those patches of random grass so beloved of town planners, an immense man wearing a hood and a long cloak. Instantly all power of movement left her: she says she felt paralysed, and with one hand still on the gate she could only stare uncomprehendingly at the gigantic, motionless figure in the direct glare of the street lamp, with his clothing moving slightly in the breeze. He appeared to be considerably over six feet tall though his height may have been exaggerated by the fact that the cloak came right to the ground completely hiding his legs and feet. The face was masked, with two narrow eye slits, but Mrs Ewing had no doubt that he was a real human being, but whether eccentric or reveller from the previous night she did not know.

Suddenly the form raised one arm in a beckoning gesture and she felt compelled to obey: her legs began to move, and with mounting fear she was drawn inexorably towards the plot of grass. Then, when

'Suddenly the form raised one arm in a beckoning gesture and she felt compelled to obey.'

she was no more than six yards from the man, with every detail now sharply clear, the figure, in her own words, 'uncannily drifted away into the grassy ground like fog'. The dreadful compulsion to go forward left her, though not the fear, but she stayed long enough to establish that there was absolutely nothing on the spot apart from the unbroken and unmarked turf. Then, very shocked, she fled towards the bus stop.

When she arrived at the hospital her colleagues were very concerned about her state of distress but were reluctant to believe her story. Later when she had recovered, she tried to find a logical reason for her experience, for never in her life had she ever considered the possibility of any contact with the supernatural. But the figure was, and remains, an enigma: not even the site could offer the slightest consolation in the form of an ancient building—prior to the development, it had been virgin gorse and scrub of the Grampians. And as there seemed to be no antecedents for the apparition, she waited apprehensively to see if it foreshadowed any event in her personal life. But again there was nothing: life has gone on ever since in the unremarkable routine of work and family. Those few intense nightmare minutes seem to have come from nowhere, to mean nothing—yet they burned themselves with indelible reality into her mind.

Mrs Gladys Ewing, Aberdeen

Non-paying Guests at the Crown Hotel

Some ghosts seem to be incredibly sensitive to change: they often emerge in a building only when a structural alteration has been made. It is difficult to assess whether the haunts have any conscious feelings or purpose, or whether they are like dust stirred up by a brush, billowing and swirling at the whim of any draught until it settles back on the floor again. A typical haunting of this type comes from the Crown Hotel in Poole, an old inn which is said to have housed at one time the notorious Judge Jeffreys when he sat at the Assizes at the Guildhall some 50 yards away. The phenomena at the Crown seems to be one of the relatively rare cases of poltergeist infestations reported recently.

In the 1960s the landlords, Alan Brown and his sister Marie Eeles, tried to attract a wider clientele by converting the upper floor of the old stable block in the courtyard into a beat club—these were the days

The piano which plays of its own accord at The Crown Hotel, Poole.

before the cheaper, simpler and now-ubiquitous discotheque. If Liverpool could achieve fame with its Cavern, what might not Poole do with its Hayloft. The juxtaposition of the up-to-date group with the antiquity of the horse age seemed a novel formula, and Mrs Eeles' 24-year-old son Paul, together with a few friends began to alter, modernise and decorate the large, low storeroom on the first floor.

About 7 June 1966 Paul and two friends, Malcolm Squire and Eric Dayman, had been working in the loft until closing time, and then came down the covered outside staircase to the yard where they stood talking to three customers from the hotel bar. Suddenly all six heard an old piano which was stored in the loft begin to play—or rather, single notes were struck one at a time as if a small child was hitting the keyboard at random with a single finger. They all laughed when Paul said that it was his ghost, and unsuspectingly trooped up the steps to see who was in the room. The whole of the loft could be seen instantly from the doorway—and it was completely empty: yet the piano continued to tinkle out a few more notes, and then fell silent. At that instant the hammers, nails and other tools which had been lying on the piano lid

The back door of the Hotel where the sounds of screaming children are heard.

shot out horizontally and fell to the floor. The six men bolted precipitately into the courtyard where they stood very frightened staring at the entrance to the stairway as if they expected some fearful apparition to emerge. When one did manifest itself it was perhaps more terrifying in that it was mysterious rather than monstrous: a ball of fluorescent mist, which Malcolm Squire with a fine sense of the macabre described as 'the size of a baby's head', drifted from the doorway, glided past the speechless little group and then floated out through the archway to vanish in Market Street.

Although Mrs Eeles complained of noises in the main inn building as if a heavy body was being dragged up and down the upper floors, the stable block remained quiet, and the three men began work again on the renovation about a week later, keeping eyes and ears alert for the first sign of the abnormal. Halfway through the evening the door of the hayloft, which had been securely fastened, swung open as the handle clicked downwards: now super-sensitive to the supernatural, Paul Eeles and his companions bolted.

Mr D Brown, an Australian who was staying in the hotel, laughed scornfully at the story with antipodean scepticism. To show Paul and his friends how their imagination had run riot he painted—for some strange reason—the offending door with five large black crosses and deliberately bolted it. He then joined the others in the courtyard. 'Then', said Mr Brown, 'I had the most eerie experience of my life— the door which I had bolted myself swung slowly wide open.' With this performance the haunt of the hayloft seemed to have exhausted itself: perhaps it was placated—or driven away—by the rhythmic beat of the groups that passed through the club soon afterwards. A strange echo of the affair however, occurred in 1975 when a milkman, who normally left the bottles at the backdoor of the inn in the courtyard between five and six in the morning, told Mrs Eeles that in future he would leave them on the pavement in the street as he was afraid of the sounds of the children whom he could hear running and screaming in the stables proper, which he knew were locked and empty.

His story made Mrs Eeles remember how years earlier she had gone out angrily because she could hear what she thought were her children at play in the stable when they should have been in bed. To her astonishment, after several ignored calls, she went to the stable, found it empty and her children already upstairs.

No clue to the origin of the strange events has been found, apart from a vague and probably contrived tale of a long-dead landlord who killed and buried two deformed children in the stable block, but an odd structural quirk in the building does start an interesting train of thought. A few years ago Mr Eeles noticed from the courtyard a small window on the fourth floor directly under the roof, which he could not account for inside the rambling passages and corridors. When he investigated with a long ladder he found that behind the window was a small room which, apart from a fireplace and a light scattering of straw on the floor was completely bare, and without any trace of a doorway.

Crown Hotel, Poole

'I Think You've Got a Poltergeist'

Poltergeists, although not reported as frequently as they used to be, remain among the longest-established and best documented of all supernatural phenomena. Yet again and again in stories of this type of haunting, both past and present, one is led to suspect that although initially the remarkable phenomena are quite spontaneous and automatic, at some stage a central figure may add some conscious assistance. If this did happen in a strange series of events at Stow-on-the-Wold between 1963 and 1965 it is very difficult to say where any dividing line could be drawn. But it does seem certain that the earlier manifestations at least were entirely genuine.

Mr Stanley Pethridge who with his wife and 14-year-old son David lived in a semi-detached house in Chapel Lane, first became aware that something mysterious was happening on 14 April 1963 when the trap-door leading to the roofspace was found out of place and cornerwise across the opening. A stepladder was brought and the trap replaced— only to be found in a diagonal position the next day. After a third displacement Mr Pethridge made an alarm with a cocoa tin and pebbles which would fall at the slightest interference: the door did not move again, but as if in annoyance that its antics had been frustrated, pools of water began to appear on the polished boards of the front hall.

The first few puddles were mopped up unquestioningly as accidents, but when it became obvious that no one in the family could have been responsible, a plumber was called in. There were no pipes in the ceiling overhead, and when the floorboards were removed it was found that there was a cavity of twelve inches below them so that seepage from the soil could be ruled out. Whether it is part of plumbers' training to offer supernatural explanations when they cannot find any faults, or whether the Stow man had a flash of inspiration is not known, but as he replaced the planks he said, 'I think you've got a poltergeist.'

Again apparently frustrated in the hall, the haunt took to flooding upstairs, and at intervals water trickled down the bedroom walls. On other occasions it dripped through the lounge ceiling until all the furniture and carpets had to be removed or covered up. On the worst day nine bowls and buckets stood on the bare floor to catch at least some of the flood that oozed from at least a dozen spots. After two months of inexplicable and intermittent inundation the first note appeared. Like the scores that followed it, it was scribbled in a large, spidery and unformed hand on scraps of paper torn from calendars, exercise books, magazines and wrapping material. The first message, which appeared to fall in front of Mrs Pethridge as she stood in the hall almost exactly on the spot where the first pool had appeared, was one of the few that was coherent: it read, 'I'll speak to you tonight.'

The Pethridges describe how when they went to bed that evening between 9.30 and 10pm a voice 'as if on a telephone from a long way away' began muttering and continued for several hours. The content was mainly gibberish, but well interlaced with swearing and obscenities, to which the Pethridges objected violently. At their request 'George' as the entity identified itself, gradually moderated its language. The muttering, like the notes which the Pethridges still keep, continued at intervals for two years, and both were varied from time to time by scribblings on the walls and ceilings, by turning off lights and television, by closing the mains water tap in the street some 20 yards away in a manhole, and by such random once-off activities as throwing marbles down the stairs and moving a heavy, oak-framed mirror from one side of the bedroom to another.

The most macabre and terrifying moment was when Mrs Pethridge went into the bedroom where David was asleep and saw emerging from under the pillow what appeared to be a baby's hand. As she watched petrified, it grew to full adult size, became gnarled and bent as if it belonged to an old man, and then vanished. All the while the stream of seemingly pointless notes with such phrases as 'going over', 'beds made', 'while it's fine', 'my real portrait', and 'don't show her none of my writing' continued to appear as did the incoherent mumblings. On occasions there were rational flashes: as Mr Pethridge was undressing one evening the disembodied voice demanded, 'What are you staring at me for, Gramp?'—'Gramp' being a pet name Mrs Pethridge sometimes used for her husband. Occasionally too, logical answers, appeared on sheets of paper on which the Pethridges had pencilled questions, though the being's concentration seemed to lapse very rapidly and after one or two replies it would slip into nonsense again. It is difficult therefore to know what significance to attach to the muttered revelation one evening that the spirit was that of a local builder who had erected the houses and had died twenty years earlier.

The case received considerable publicity in the national press at the time and it was hinted that David was responsible for at least some of the more blatant manifestations. Mr and Mrs Pethridge say that one very large circulation Sunday paper offered them £5,000 if they would confirm that their son was behind the hauntings, but despite this very tempting offer they refused, pointing out that on many occasions when the notes or the voice (the most suspect features of the case) appeared, David had not been in the house at all. A local vicar, Canon Cheales, who witnessed many of the phenomena himself, is still utterly convinced that they were genuinely supernatural.

In classical poltergeist tradition the manifestations gradually subsided until by 1965 they had gone altogether. Today, in their home in Chapel Lane, Mr and Mrs Pethridge have only some saw marks on the hall floor, a large packet of fading pencilled notes and press cuttings, and a very puzzled memory to remind them of the disturbing events of 1963 and 1964.

Mr Pethridge, Gloucestershire

The Naked Embrace

Rural East Anglia at its most commonplace seems a haunted region: grey Constable clouds bank up over a grey flat landscape, while the sparse trees moan in the cutting wind that seems perpetually to stream from the cold grey north. It is little wonder that the eastern counties are peopled at every turn by phantoms: even if there were no history or tradition one can conjure them up from the very atmosphere of the place. And of nowhere is this more true than Langenhoe in Essex.

But from 1937 to 1959 Langenhoe did not need imaginary ghosts, because the church and the manor house, which stood side by side on the desolate marshes a mile from the village, were the scene of a remarkable and varied display of psychic phenomena. In 1937 Rev Ernest Merryweather was appointed rector after a number of incumbencies in the north of England, where he had had no experience of the supernatural nor showed any interest in it. But within a few weeks of arriving at Langenhoe he was immersed in a series of strange events that lasted until he retired 22 years later. At first these seemed typical poltergeist pranks—doors in the church slammed with explosive violence on days of dead calm; the rector's valise locked itself in the vestry and refused to open until it was well outside the walls; flowers placed on the altar or elsewhere in the building moved from place to place or vanished completely. There were steady reports of the classical thuds on doors, sharp cracks and the automatic ringing of the credence bell by the altar. Once Mr Merryweather and several parishioners heard the sound of an old man coughing from the bricked-up doorway that had once been the entrance for the manor family.

Then, in 1947, the manifestations took a much more concrete form. Mr Merryweather was being shown over the manor house by its owner, who, on reaching one bedroom said that she did not use it as it always felt uncanny. The lady moved on but the rector paused to admire the wonderful view from the window, and then turning to follow, he was suddenly overwhelmed by the sensation of being embraced by a naked young woman: nothing was seen, heard or smelt—only the tactile impression for a few seconds of soft arms, soft breasts and body pressed against him. This experience, about which the rector was most emphatic, is extremely rare: tactile psychic sensations are almost invariably the more unpleasant ones of choking, pressure or restriction.

A year later the basic femininity of the haunt revealed itself again. Mr Merryweather who because of an outbreak of hooliganism had brought an ornamental dagger to church with him, felt it snatched from his belt as he stood at the altar and simultaneously heard a woman's voice from the tower end of the building cry, 'You are a cruel man.'

The overgrown graveyard of Langenhoe.

In August 1949 the phantom at last became visible: in the middle of a communion service the rector suddenly glanced up from the gospel to see a woman aged about 30, and to all intents a living person, dressed in a long white dress with flowing headgear, move across the chancel and disappear through the solid wall of the south-west corner. Later, a photograph showing the damage done to the church by the earthquake of 1884 revealed that a hitherto unsuspected doorway had once existed in this part of the fabric.

In September 1950 the ghost, having displayed audible, tactile and visual manifestations began another approach, and filled the church with a powerful smell of violets, long out of season. But this was a once-only experiment, and though a female form was seen in the building in July 1951 and October 1952, the majority of subsequent phenomena were auditory. Late in 1950, when the rector was standing in the vestry he heard clearly a female voice chanting plain song. A week later he found two workmen peering through the keyhole of the locked church and wondering how the sound of a group of people singing in French could come from a place they knew was empty. On another occasion Mr Merryweather arriving alone, and standing in the entrance heard a muttered conversation in the chancel, with a man's voice raised but undecipherable. As he entered the church there was an unhappy sigh, then silence.

A very strong local tradition tells of a woman murdered by an earlier rector who had become her lover, but while this may be true, it looks suspiciously like creating a story to fit the facts. It has been said too that the whole affair was in the mind of Mr Merryweather—but it seems strange that in his long life this level-headed and cheerful man who was happily married with several children, should never have experienced anything except in the church itself and once in the manor. The church was closed in 1959 and completely demolished three years later: all that remains today is a small field ringed with gravestones, eerily overgrown with brambles as if for some macabre film set, and leaning at different angles towards the crowded empty space of open turf in the centre where the haunted building once stood.

Collated from diverse sources

One More Than Fate

In many villages the manor house stands next to the church: in more pious days with frequent obligatory services, this was probably for the convenience of the local lord. But many later squires whose life style was the envy of the villagers, even if the bane of the vicar, must have found the proximity unsettling. The morning clangour of bells 20 yards from the bedroom window must have vibrated cords of conscience in the heart of many a gentleman bleary from a night of liquor or lechery.

The manor house at Denton, near Newhaven in Sussex is unusually close to the church—a footpath and just enough room for a double row of graves separates the out walls of the two buildings. It was built as a prosperous farmhouse of some fourteen rooms and a gloomy cellar in 1724, and whatever its past, today its proximity to the church is very much a matter of practical convenience because since 1973 it has been the rectory. Exactly forty years earlier, however, in a very different context, it achieved considerable notoriety.

In September 1933 Mr and Mrs King moved in with their 12-year-old daughter and Mrs King's elderly mother, Mrs Heasman, and until November relaxed in the rural peace. The ghostly campaign against the Kings opened, as so many do, with a single loud crash in an upper room, as if a piece of heavy furniture had fallen over. Of course nothing was found wrong, and the Kings dismissed the incident as strange but not alarming. Events of the following Sunday made them change their minds.

As Mrs King was walking along an upstairs corridor—which like

The rectory at Denton.

most of the house is even today much as it was in the eighteenth
century—she was suddenly faced with a phantom figure whose
appearance was so vague that it was impossible even to decide its sex.
For all that, however, it was terrifying, and Mrs King's screams
brought her husband running from a bedroom, waving a stick he had
grabbed on the way. He too saw the apparition, and hit out at it, but the
blow passed through airy nothingness and gouged a groove in the
plaster of the wall as the shadowy form faded from sight. As the figure
vanished, four thunderous crashes reverberated through the house.
For the next four or five days these were repeated with uncanny and
frightening regularity, usually at twenty to, or twenty past the hour, at
five-hourly intervals, as if some psychic battery were charging up
slowly and then discharging itself in one terrible burst. The sounds
seemed to come from somewhere near the centre of the building but
could be heard all over the house and even outside in the garden and
lane: as the time for the next manifestation approached, tension grew
unbearable, especially for Mrs King.

After three days of unremitting pressure, the rector, Rev E Pinnix
was called in and though after hearing the noises he said prayers, the

102

spirit which had brought Mrs King almost to the point of collapse, and the family to the point of leaving, was not going to be deterred by an unofficial exorcism, so that the quadruple bombardment went on unabated. That night, however, the family went to sleep at a house a quarter of a mile away leaving the manor under the watchful ears and eyes of a policeman and a crowd of local people. The vigil was not unrewarded: at 10.20pm came the vengeful knocks, and when the constable and several members of the crowd went inside nothing was found, although one of the searchers claims to have heard, or sensed, someone rushing past him in the darkness.

The following day the Kings began packing, and a reporter from the *Brighton Evening Argus* standing amidst the crates and confusion reported: 'I heard the noise myself. I was standing in one of the rooms talking to the rector when suddenly, from the direction of the scullery, there came the sound of four distinct knockings, followed by a shriek from Mrs King . . . ' The reporter also commented on the cellar door which, bolted a few moments earlier, was now wide open although no one had been near it. The King family left the house for good on Thursday: for the next few nights crowds estimated by some local people at hundreds arrived on foot, by car and even by coach to wait in the darkened lane in the hope of some manifestation. There seems to have been no performance on the first two evenings but those who braved the cold dampness of a late November Saturday night—were suddenly chilled by four sudden and loud bangs from inside the empty house. Many waited until well after midnight, but nothing but their own footsteps and whisperings, and the distant hiss of the sea broke the stillness: they had heard the last performance. The old manor house today, says the rector's wife, despite its rambling inconvenience and lofty coldness, radiates only exceptional peace and happiness.

Local tradition, which always dislikes untidy ends and unresolved problems, tried to find a logical cause for the Denton haunting, and decided that the apparition was that of a Miss Catt of Bishopstone, a former owner of the house, who resented the fact that Mr King had felled two trees in the garden which she had planted. But this solution seems too facile, and it may be that the haunting was a poltergeist manifestation, centred on the Kings' daughter.

Collated from diverse sources

Something Evil

For years after 1945 the painfully-slow progress up the housing lists preoccupied the minds of tens of thousands of families even more than it does today. As through the 1950s the building progamme staggered under the weight of shortages, priorities and political pressures, many councils bought older property, modernised it as far as they could and let it to those most in need.

Number 32 Coxwell Road, Birmingham was one such house: in a faceless row built about the turn of the century for 'respectable' artisans, it might not, even with its new mod cons be the ultimate in luxury, but compared with the squalor of the condemned premises in which Frank Pells and his family had been compelled to live for two years, it was a palace. By the time they moved in in May 1955 a fifth child had been born and when Father Etherington, their local priest, blessed the house, gleaming in its new utility paint, they felt that all the struggle and waiting had not been wasted. But within a week, the family was faced with a minor puzzle: everyone in the house was awakened by the violent slamming of doors, which when checked, were found to be still securely fastened. Inexplicable tapping noises came from the bedroom ceilings, and from time to time the house was permeated with an overpowering smell which seemed to begin as garlic and then gradually transform itself into burning rubber.

Frank Pells, an ex-paratrooper with 40 drops, many of them on active service, was not the man to be intimidated by such distractions: he and his wife decided that though odd, these trivial disadvantages were infinitesimal compared with the advantages of a sound, three-bedroom house at a reasonable rent. Three weeks later the first body blow fell: the month-old baby was found dead in the bed where it slept with its parents. The post-mortem showed suffocation, but Mrs Pells had reservations because she felt that had either of them lain on the child it would have shown some sign. As good catholics they were comforted by the hope of resurrection and determined to re-create happiness round the rest of the family and their new home.

But as so often happens with hauntings, the intensity of the manifestations began to increase as if some malign spirit had sensed victory. Rappings in the ceiling above the kitchen, heard by relatives and friends as well as by the Pells, began regularly at about 10.20pm: the door slamming sounds were consistent although everything was checked before the family went to bed. The temperature of the room above the kitchen changed almost hourly, and the strange variable odours filled all corners of the house. Far more disturbing was a new manifestation in the form of menacing whispering of indistinguishable words, rather like someone whispering into a microphone.

A few days after the baby's death 4-year-old Alan asked, 'Did baby go away with the little white dog?' Terrified, Mrs Pells asked, 'What dog?' The lad replied, 'The little white dog that comes and sits on my bed. I saw him sitting on baby's face the night baby went away.' Mrs Pells collapsed. The police were sent for to deal with a dog unlikely to be real, and Father Etherington to take care of a more probable ghostly one. The police found nothing: the priest, assisted by a relative of the Pells, Joe Neill, sprinkled his holy water, and both men heard the rapping and the sibilant whispering. Father Etherington advised the Pells to leave the house at once, but the journey to Coxwell Road had been such a bitter one, they did not wish to have to cover the ground again. A fortnight later, however, had the road been to Golgotha, they might well have chosen it.

Frank Pells was downstairs shaving at the kitchen sink when the terrible jibbering began right behind him: there was obviously no one there, and the only other person in the house was his wife, who was in the bedroom. He rushed to the stairs: at the top stood his wife, her face distorted with terror and her mouth obviously screaming, though no sound reached him. Frank Pells dashed up the stairs towards her, but halfway up he hit an invisible barrier that pushed him back. He seized the bannisters with both hands, and pulling and thrusting with all his considerable strength, he burst through: instantly he could hear his wife's sobs and cries. She too had heard the frightening, threatening mutterings. They left the house at once, not waiting even to pack or make the beds. Mr Pells' niece and her fiance volunteered to return to clear up, but a single evening was enough: the constant whisperings and noises drove them away with the vow they would never go back.

The council, convinced that the Pells were convinced, rehoused them immediately. A reporter from a national paper and his photographer spent a night in the house, and though there was no spectral form to photograph, nor phantom noises to record, they did confirm that there were very definite fluctuations of temperature and strange smells that came and went. Whatever inhabited 32 Coxwell Road for the early summer of 1955 may have been a completely random entity, or it may have had particular malice towards the Pells. Certainly all is silent there today.

Collated from diverse sources

The Invisible Mauler

From 1947 until 1950 Victor and Betty Sargent, and later their son Christopher, had lived miserably in rooms, forced to use other people's belongings at highly inflated prices. Then in April 1950 they found in Epsom a bright, self-contained flat whose two bedrooms, lounge and kitchen now made all the waiting seem worth-while. But the fact that two months later they were back again living in a single room in Sheen Park, Richmond with Mr Sargent spending an hour travelling to work instead of a few minutes, indicates the extent of their terror of the flat.

The first intimation that the place had a sinister and invisible tenant

'Something began pulling at her shoulders, dragging her in the direction of the windows.'

came soon after they moved in: about 11pm Betty Sargent heard a tapping at the head of her bed and then something in the darkness touched her forehead. To find something—a mouse or a bird perhaps—would have been disturbing enough, but to switch on the light and after a long search find nothing, was much more alarming.

With its presence announced, the poltergeist or whatever the force was, lay quiet for a few days, but the following week began in earnest. During the daytime it concentrated on what it must have considered its more playful tricks, such as throwing pyjamas on the floor, disturbing the carefully made beds, and upsetting the cosmetics. It began to indicate its more vicious side when it ripped open the cellophane packet of a pair of new nylons—still a rare luxury—and tossed them on the floor, hopelessly laddered.

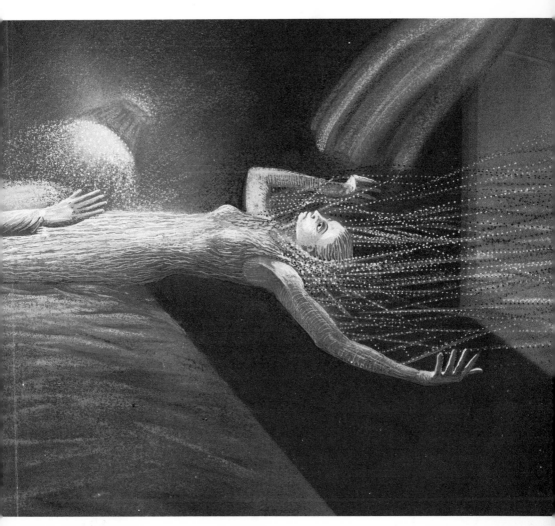

But the entity became really vindictive and vigorous in the hour before, and the hour after midnight, and brought the Sargent family to desperation through sheer mental and physical terror. One night, Mrs Sargent was torn, almost hysterical, from a deep sleep by invisible hands clutching at her throat: when she and her husband fled bewildered to the lounge to lie down on the settee, the strangling sensation began again. Victor described how a few nights later they were lying in bed as midnight approached when he saw a small lamp beside his wife's bed rise in the air, strike her on the forehead and then pass on to fall near him.

It was not long after this there came the incident that convinced them that the evil presence was no longer content merely to terrify them, but was threatening their lives physically. Betty Sargent was sitting up in bed when something, presumably the hands that had tried to throttle her, began pulling on her shoulders, dragging her in the direction of the window. As she screamed for help her body was held horizontal, her legs and thighs only resting on the bed. Victor grabbed her, but the inexorable force began to pull him too towards the window. Suddenly, the power collapsed, and Betty fell to the floor: they believed there had been a deliberate intent to kill, for had not her husband been present, Mrs Sargent might easily have fallen to what would have been assumed was a suicide death. Within a few days they were huddled in one room, a dozen miles away.

So far as is known the flat has remained quiet ever since, and one can only speculate on the nature of the malevolence that seemed to have a personal grudge against Mrs Sargent: she herself feels that if such forces can have gender, this one must have been feminine. Nothing else, she says, could be so utterly catty.

Betty Sargent, Epsom

The Unexplained

Apparitions from the Moors

The fear that the incomplete corpse is earthbound and wanders as a restless spirit, searching, searching, is as old as mankind itself. Equally ancient is the terror of the disturbed grave: there seems an almost instinctive belief that the broken rest of the body in some ways destroys the peace of the spirit, which must return once more to earth, often to seek revenge. Perhaps it was this that occurred in the moorland village of Chipping in north Lancashire in 1966.

Leagram Hall, Chipping, the ancestral home of the Weld family, had by 1963 fallen into such a state that it was entirely uneconomic to repair and was demolished. The coffins from the vault in the family chapel were removed to the nearby Catholic churchyard—an event which, it was said locally, 'upset the ancestors no end to be among ordinary people.' Not surprisingly in view of expectations, on top of a centuries-old tradition of hauntings, 'events' began almost immediately. Cars were reported to have stopped inexplicably in the lane which skirted the estate and would not restart; figures leapt from the bank right into the path of moving vehicles, which went right through them; sounds, mists and the whole range of psychic phenomena were claimed. With the supernatural always good copy the press and TV soon converged on Chipping, but as usual the phantoms disdained to display themselves for vulgar entertainment. The media soon tired of the futile pursuit and as the light of publicity turned elsewhere, so did the fickle public. The ancestors, if indeed they were responsible, seemed to have accepted their status and position in the modern world and to have resumed their centuries-old sleep.

There was, however, a dramatic revival: a few days before Christmas 1966 Madge Kenyon, whose family for at least three generations had been estate agents at the hall, and her 16-year-old daughter Mollie, set out along the deserted lane that led from the village past the site of the old mansion towards the moors taking their miniature poodle for its usual run. It was shortly after 4pm, with the dusk settling down in misty anticipation of Christmas. At around 4.30, when they were about half a mile from the village, the Kenyons decided that as they had done nothing towards preparing the family supper they must return home and were just about to do so when both simultaneously saw three figures approaching them from the direction of the moor. Because of the fading light the people appeared at first to be little more than sil-houettes but soon they were clearly distinguishable as a woman and two boys aged about ten and twelve. This seemed enough to identify them as a farming family the Kenyons knew slightly and who would certainly want to stop and talk: conscious of a homecoming husband and an unprepared meal, Madge Kenyon wanted to avoid them but did not want to appear rude by turning about so abruptly that the reason was obvious.

Her dilemma was, however, resolved in a surprising way: the village postmistress' dog Sam, who normally accompanied them on their walks but who that afternoon had missed them as they passed his home, shot round the bend, excited and delighted to have found them. The Kenyons' attention was diverted for a few moments from the approaching trio by Sam's cavortings, and when they looked up again the woman and her sons were only a few yards away although neither Madge nor her daughter had heard a single footstep.

Mrs Kenyon had time only to notice that the newcomers were complete strangers and not the family she had expected when a dramatic change in Sam's behaviour demanded her whole attention: he crouched on his stomach with fangs bared and hair bristling as he fixed his eyes on the strangers, snarling savagely. Sam, who was normally the most amiable of beasts, so alarmed Madge that she turned back to the woman and her children to explain that they need not be afraid as the dog was quite harmless—and found the road completely empty. The family who seconds earlier had been standing no more than a couple of yards away had vanished: there was no possibility they had gone on because visibility was still reasonable, and in any case their movement would have been noticed.

The disappearance of the three figures had a traumatic effect on Sam: suddenly in desperation he leaped forward exactly as if he were in a fight, snarling, snapping the air, ducking, weaving as he now attacked, now retreated from an invisible enemy. The Kenyons' own dog crept closely between them, and stood trembling in every fibre. Then abruptly in what seemed to be a particularly vicious phase of the battle, Sam was utterly defeated: turning in ignominious flight with his tail tucked between his legs he made a frantic swerve as if to avoid some force attacking his flank and broke away rushing headlong down the lane, howling pitifully.

Absolutely bewildered by the unexpectedness and speed of the whole incident the Kenyons stared at the dog as it raced towards the village, screaming and beside itself with terror: then as they peered into

'The three figures materialised about ten yards away waving their arms threateningly as they chased the dog.'

110

The 'new' grave of the Weld family.

the grey dusk where an instant before there had been nothing but an empty lane and incipient night, the three figures materialised about 10 yards away, waving their arms threateningly as they chased the fleeing Sam. Whether it was reality, or whether a trick of the half light, the gruesome trio now seemed larger than when they had been near at hand. Mother and daughter watched horrified and speechless as the dog and the ghastly apparitions disappeared round a bend in the track. It was only when everything had vanished from sight that they spoke— and then only to confirm that they had both seen the same nightmare scene. It was then too that they realised that they had the worse ordeal to come, because the phantoms were now between them and the village.

But the journey back was something of an anti-climax: there was nothing but the deepening dusk and their own footsteps on the way back to Chipping—except that their own dog, instead of his normal

The lane where the apparitions were seen.

random rushings to and fro, shrank between the two women, his nose touching Madge's leg at every step as if to reassure himself that she at least was mortal. In the village, they rushed home, too afraid even to stop at the post office to ask if Sam had reached safety. 'I was,' says Madge, 'past explaining.'

A few days later when she heard that the dog was very ill she regretted her cowardice. The vet was certain that there was nothing organically wrong: it just seemed, he said, as if the animal had given up the will to live. A week later it was dead, responding to no drugs and rejecting all help. 'I told the post office people,' says Madge, 'and they believed me, but it was no use saying that to the vet.'

For a long time the Kenyons refused to use the lane in case the terrible silent family was still vengefully stalking it, but as the immediate fear subsided, once more they resumed their usual walk, though it was many months before their own dog would accompany them again. But never since, though Madge has passed the spot hundreds of times, both alone and with others, has she felt even a trace of the weird events of that December afternoon.

Mrs Madge Kenyon, Lancashire

The Silent Procession

A few miles from Accrington comes another strange haunting which has a disturbing similarity to the one in the Mackey home. Mr Stephen Wood describes an experience he had as a small boy in 1957 in Great Harwood, a town less than three miles from Accrington, and on the very edge of what was once the great Pendle Forest. While a single sighting by a child might easily be dismissed (as it was at the time) as a dream or a fantasy, taken in conjunction with the totally illogical apparition seen by Carole Mackey, it must be considered seriously—an attitude reinforced by the complete conviction and sincerity with which Mr Wood writes.

In 1957 the Wood family were living in a council house in Burns Way, Great Harwood, a house built about ten years earlier and in which, as far as anyone knows, no event of any violence had taken place. Stephen's bedroom, from which there was a clear view to Pendle Hill, contained little except two single beds, one on each side of the small fireplace with their heads against the shorter wall.

One night in October, rather unusually because he was normally a very sound sleeper, Stephen woke up. He did not know the time, but as there was no sound either from his own home or outside, it must have been well after midnight. The room was not in impenetrable darkness because of the diffused light of the moon; it was the kind of blackness which allows familiar objects to be seen, perhaps more with memory's eye than with real vision, and which makes the unfamiliar ones vague patches against the gloom.

Suddenly, to his astonishment—the event was so incredible that fear took some time to develop—he saw the silhouettes of five figures moving silently and apparently without any movement of limbs from the fireplace near his head to the wall at the opposite end of the room. The figures were, as accurately as Stephen can remember, about three feet high, and although no clothing as such was distinguishable, they seemed to be solid down to the floor. They showed no sign of hair so that the sharp round outline of the heads together with their darkness gave Stephen the impression that they were negroes. If black can glow, he said, then these did, for the inky shapes stood out clearly from the

Stephen Wood working on one of his paintings.

darkness of the bedroom. As the astounded boy watched the procession, which moved now slowly, now quickly, they came to the wall beyond his feet. Here, he saw with dawning fear, sat a sixth figure, featureless, and opaque like the others but with an indeterminate shadow which might have been a hat, a crown or a mitre on its head. As each of the phantoms in the procession reached the figure which was raised above the floor, it handed up a 'present', which Stephen says might have been a jug, and then made its way back down the room, past its companions to the fireplace where it began its journey once more.

Now petrified the boy called quietly but desperately to his sister who was in the other bed a few feet away: she was, apparently, soundly asleep and made no answer, but all the time the shining blackness of the

The five figures moved silently from the fireplace to the opposite end of the room.

115

*Painting by Stephen Wood in the style suggested to him
by his childhood vision.*

silhouettes slid up and down the bedroom with their offerings. Then, quite suddenly, all faded: there was just the empty night tinged with a touch of greyness from the clouded moon. The irresistible demands of sleep which can transcend fear and excitement once more claimed him, but in the morning every detail of the strange experience was as vivid as it had been in the darkness.

His story was, inevitably, attributed to a dream, but Stephen, who now after twenty years remembers every instant with frozen clarity, believes differently. Never since has he seen anything vaguely resembling the apparition of that night, nor has he had any further kind of psychic experience—unless, of course, you consider his paintings. Stephen is an artist in his spare time, and in a postscript to one of his letters writes: 'While writing this letter something has come to me that you might like to know. All my pictures seem to be of silhouettes against the sunset. I had not thought about it until just now. I wonder if my early experience has anything to do with the way I paint?'

Stephen Wood, Blackburn

118

Sense of Evil

It seems that sometimes the most puzzling and most mysterious supernatural happenings have the most ordinary and normal of settings. Certainly there was no long family history at 38 Pendle Street, Accrington, nor, as far as is known, any powerful emotional occurrences other than the natural and expected births and deaths. Yet this little two-up-two-down-no-garden house was the setting for a macabre and well-authenticated haunting lasting several years.

Mr and Mrs Mackey and their three children, Carole, Gary and Janice, aged thirteen, eleven and six respectively when the events began, were as normal as their surroundings even if Carole did have a tendency to sleepwalking. This was, however, of a minor nature and she invariably woke up at the top of the stairs or when she was a few steps down them. On one occasion in April 1965 there was an exception. Carole had almost reached the hall at the bottom of the stairs before she was aware what was happening: immediately she was fully conscious she felt the tomb-like silence and blackness of the early hours of the morning, and the next instant an overwhelming but intangible sense of evil and danger that had never accompanied any previous waking. Terrified, and hoping that the awful sensation would vanish if she shut out the impenetrable darkness round her, she closed her eyes, but a moment later hearing a faint sound in the lobby, she opened them again.

This ordinary-looking house was the scene of one of England's most bizarre hauntings.

Instantly, almost before she could see, she experienced a wave of intense heat—most unusual in psychic phenomena, which seem to have a predilection for chills. Then in absolute terror she saw a glowing formless shape about human size 'standing' no more than a yard in front of her. It had, she says, a face, yet no face: there were features which she knew in some non-sensible way were male, yet which were in constant flux, flowing evilly from one character to another, but all the time projecting an inexpressible hatred. Carole was conscious that it reached the floor so that as she was standing on the second or third step its face was on a level with hers staring straight at her. But she could not be certain of any specific limbs in the amoeba-like, changing flow in front of her. Only the 'head' and 'shoulders' amorphous though these were, held any consistent identity.

For the first instant it was the sheer ugliness of the apparition that froze all her senses, and after this, the transcending malevolence that it seemed to bear towards her personally. Had she not by chance stopped immediately opposite the light switch it is difficult to know what might have happened, but as she pressed it, flooding the hall with light, the vision vanished. Petrified, she went back to bed, not daring to say anything. The experience was so incredible that she was sure it would be met with ridicule or punishment.

A few weeks afterwards Carole was wakened by the sound of something falling heavily from a chair in the room below her, and then the noise of dragging and a peculiar rhythmic scratching. Thinking that it was the family poodle who slept in the room needing to go outside, she went downstairs. The regular scratching continued in the darkness but the moment she put on the light it ceased. The dog, she was scared to see, was soundly asleep, and the blanket which covered it was undisturbed.

Mystified she went back to bed. In the months that followed she heard the same sequence of sounds on a number of occasions. Once she approached the living room door and called quietly into the darkness: the dog at once roused itself from sleep and padded eagerly towards her, but above the pitter-patter of its paws she could hear the continuing rhythm of the scratching.

In the spring of 1966 Gary, who slept downstairs, confided to Carole that he often got up in the night to see what was the matter with the dog as he kept hearing a bump and an odd scratching noise. The only trouble, he said, was that whenever he went into the living room the poodle was soundly asleep and had apparently been so all night. When she said that she too had heard similar noises, Gary was prompted to a further confidence: on several occasions, he said, when he had got up in

'She saw a glowing, formless shape about human size "standing" no more than a yard in front of her.'

121

Carole Chadwick.

the darkness he had seen a vaguely round, but changing, ball of light floating round the living room, but this had vanished the moment he switched on the lamps.

The haunting at the Mackey home is so bizarre that it would be difficult to know where to start to find antecedents, but it might be worth remembering that Pendle has a significant place in the history of the occult in England. Pendle Street, Accrington is only a stone's throw from the once-notorious Pendle Forest, the great centre of witchcraft in the country in the sixteenth century. It was here that nine witches out of twenty charged were executed in 1612, and another seventeen sentenced to death in 1633, though these were eventually reprieved by Charles I after suffering the most terrible torments.

Mrs Carole Chadwick, Blackburn

'The Baby's Dead, I tell you, the Baby's Dead'

The sheer arbitrariness of some psychic phenomena is one of the strengths for belief in the unknown—the very triviality of the events gives them the stamp of authenticity. Over the years Howard Glansfield of Kettering has had a number of experiences, many of them so slight that taken in isolation they could be regarded as coincidences, accidents or imagination, but their consistency builds up an impressive case. One incident which happened in 1962, a few months after his marriage, seems on the surface so pointless that no one would have bothered to invent it, or recall it, unless it had been utterly sincere.

Howard had been taken by his wife to visit her elderly great aunt who lived in Birmingham. There were no particularly deep bonds between the two women, indeed, even among closer relatives Aunt Sophie was a remote and unknown figure, but it was in the family tradition of courtesy to introduce a new member. Suddenly, in the middle of a polite conversation Howard felt compelled to ask where the dog was. There was no indication in the room that the old lady had ever owned a pet of any sort, but she did look slightly shocked. Howard then felt his gaze drawn to one corner of the room, and as he stared the apparition of a small terrier began to appear. The animal sat quite still, though apparently alive, for several minutes while Howard described it aloud in detail. Aunt Sophie seemed very moved and said that every detail corresponded with a dog she had had some thirty years earlier and which had always sat on that spot when she played the piano. Although the visible form faded, Howard said that he was very conscious of the animal's presence in the room for the whole of the time they were there.

Years later the Glansfields, now with two children, spent five summer holidays in succession at a remote cottage near Sarnau, Cardiganshire which had once been a farmhouse. For the first four of those years it was perfect: in beautiful and peaceful country-side with the unspoiled coast only a few miles away it seemed the ideal retreat for a young family. But in 1974, as they unloaded the car at the cottage full of anticipation of another delightful holiday, they realised that something had changed. Both Mr and Mrs Glansfield sensed an indefinable and hostile atmosphere, though neither of them mentioned it until the events which forced the deepest confidences later.

On the very first day in the cottage Howard experienced a longing to play an organ which he felt should be in the front living room but which, of course, was not there. Although he played the piano at home for amusement he had never until that moment showed the slightest interest in the organ, but in the days that followed, the desire became almost unbearable. When he mentioned the seemingly pointless sensation to the owner, who had been brought up in the cottage when it was the farmhouse, he was told that when the place had been the family home, a harmonium, naturally used only for hymns, had always stood in the room.

After this gentle and almost amusing brush with the supernatural, events took a more sinister turn. Mr and Mrs Glansfield were using for the first time the most comfortable front bedroom—a room which in previous visits they had hospitably allocated to friends and guests—when in the early hours of the morning Mrs Glansfield woke with dismay to hear the unmistakable sound of someone, possibly a child, she thought, being beaten with a whip or strap. There were no cries of pain, nothing visible—only the rhythmic thudding and swish, and at the same time an intense sensation of pain.

She slipped from bed and crept to the door to investigate, but the sounds ceased abruptly. And as they did so she became aware of a new noise—a gasping for breath from the room where her eldest son was sleeping. Rushing in she found him in the throes of his first attack of asthma, and although both she and her husband tried to dismiss the incident as a confusion of sounds in the darkness, they knew that the apprehension they had experienced in the first few minutes in the cottage had not been mistaken. Two or three days later Howard, soundly asleep, heard a child's voice sobbing 'Mummy, the baby's crying, Mummy, the baby's crying.' He woke up, considered briefly, and dismissed what he thought was a typical random and pointless dream, when to his absolute astonishment he saw at the end of the room a woman and a small child. The woman repeated tonelessly 'The baby's dead, I tell you, the baby's dead.' The two figures faded leaving Howard very disturbed but what he felt at the time was nothing to his reaction when at breakfast time his son asked, 'Who was the little girl you were talking to in the middle of the night, daddy?' The boy had apparently wakened up and had heard the voices.

Towards the end of their stay came the final manifestation that convinced the Glansfields that despite its many advantages, and the delightful times they had had there, they could never return to the cottage. Mrs Glansfield was wakened by the sensation of a cat's fur brushing her face, and in the panic that so often accompanies the unexpected waking by an outside agency, she sat bolt upright in bed. There, at the foot, and leaning over the bottom rail, was a woman whose description tallied exactly with that seen by Howard a few days earlier. She appeared to be between 35 and 45 years old with a work-worn face and greying hair pulled back into a coiled bun. She was dressed all in bluish-grey, and with precise detail Mrs Glansfield remembers the blouse with pin tucks, long sleeves and pearl buttons, and the coarse skirt whose length she could not judge because the lower third of the figure was hidden by the bed. The apparition looked hard at Mrs Glansfield with an expression of profound sadness, and then slowly faded.

Mr Glansfield tried hard in the remaining days to find out about any events that might have caused the haunting, but the locals, like local people everywhere who do not wish to give anything away, fell into silence—or here into the much more effective alternative, Welsh. The only hint—and that a very vague one—was that in the 1920s there had been a still birth in the house. If this were true, might not the pathetic shadow have been attracted by young children in the house, perhaps in envy, perhaps in vicarious joy in a son like the one she had lost.

H Glansfield, Kettering

The Uninvited Guest

A building on which some psychic energy is centred can sometimes display a wide variety of manifestations. This seems most commonly the case with poltergeists, and may, or may not, be the reason behind a strange series of hauntings in a large early-Victorian house in Coventry between 1972 and 1974.

The building, in the rambling style of an earlier age, was too large even for the Harris family, Jane and Leslie and their five children. As a result, as soon as they bought it in 1972 they let some of the rooms as furnished accommodation, but soon became a little disturbed by the turnover of tenants, some of whom left at a minute's notice after complaining of inexplicable noises and sensations. The Harrises themselves were aware of these sounds which consisted of thudding on floors and ceilings, heavy breathing and what appeared to be footsteps. Though these sounds were experienced fairly generally throughout the house, they were most evident in the bedroom used by Mr and Mrs Harris and those adjacent to it.

Initially Mr Harris put these disturbances down to structural movements in the old building, but soon there were events which could not be laid so easily at the door of creaking timbers and crumbling brickwork. The first tangible incident occurred in mid-1972 when Jane Harris had gone to bed early leaving Leslie downstairs watching television. Some time later he was alarmed by a piercing scream which sent him dashing upstairs to find his wife frantically trying to claw something invisible from her face. When he had pacified her into coherency she explained that she had fallen asleep, but had been suddenly wakened by the terrifying sensation of fur being pressed over her nose and mouth, stifling her. They discussed the affair as rationally as they could against the background of the mysterious sounds that had been reported, but half decided that it must have been a nightmare.

However, they began to have second thoughts a few weeks later when in the middle of the night their bedroom door burst open and a terrified lodger, Ann Turner, threw herself on their bed. When she had been quietened she said that she could stay in the house no longer: for some weeks, she explained, she had been alarmed by the sound of footsteps entering her room in the night and by deep breathing at the side of her bed, but that night someone had tried to suffocate her by pressing fur over her face. Miss Turner left and two Americans who were quite unaware of any previous happenings in the house took over her room; after a few weeks they too announced at breakfast that they would be leaving instantly as they could no longer stand the footsteps and breathing of something invisible that entered their locked room during the night.

The knockings under the floor of the Harrises' own bedroom increased in intensity gradually, and Leslie, still perhaps hoping to find a physical explanation, had the boards taken up. But the timberwork underneath was as sound as the day it had been put in, and there was no sign of anything that could have caused even a creaking, much less the heavy pounding that was now disturbing them. The only discovery was a small framed oil painting, covered in dust and cobwebs, concealed in the cavity between the floor and the ceiling of the downstairs room. The picture had become so dark that detail was almost indistinguishable, but a man standing by a tree near the banks of a river could just be made out. The painting, found to be by an early nineteenth-century French artist, was subsequently sold at Christies in 1973. Why it was hidden was never found out, but its discovery, far from placating whatever was causing the noises, seemed to have annoyed it for although the floor now remained silent the hammering from the ceiling and from a mirror on the wall increased alarmingly. Not surprisingly, tension in the house mounted.

The first intimation that there might be a definite identity behind the manifestations came some weeks later when Jane Harris woke up wanting to go to the bathroom, but in view of all that had happened was reluctant to do so on her own. She sat up in bed; noted that the time was exactly three o'clock, and then listened intently, partly for the frightening rapping, but also for any sound from the room above where 14-year-old David slept. Soon after coming to the house David had suddenly and mysteriously started walking in his sleep. But footsteps, phantom and physical were silent. Then out of the darkness she heard a woman's voice calling very softly, 'David . . . David . . .' Its source was difficult to pinpoint—it seemed to come from everywhere with its seductive and insistent 'David . . . David . . .' Frantic, Jane woke her husband up and cried, 'She's calling him . . . she's calling him,' almost as if at the back of her mind she knew that the presence in the house was feminine.

Leslie sat up beside her, straining his ears in the stillness. He had just said that it was all imagination when they heard a muffled thud above them and then the slow shuffling steps of a somnambulist. They both raced to the top floor, where they found David groping his way along the corridor, so deeply asleep that they could not waken him. Gently they guided him back to his room and bed.

As if gaining in confidence, moving from random sounds to speech, the haunt at last showed itself in visible manifestation. One evening in the early winter of 1974 Jane backed the car down the drive towards the main road, but as she reached the gateway she glanced back at the house and noticed that someone had arrived at the front door. She drove the car back, got out and approached the visitor, who, she was surprised to see, was a complete stranger. She appeared to be in her early twenties, with a very unfashionable long dark dress and a small white cap or hat on her head. Her hair was drawn back, and as Jane came near she could see that the woman seemed to be utterly miserable. Thinking that she was perhaps lost, and rather concerned about her distress, Jane went to see if she could help but to her amazement when she was about three yards away, the woman slowly faded, leaving the front path and doorstep eerily empty in the brightness of the street lighting.

Events were now moving towards a climax, which was precipitated when Jane heard one of the tenants talking to her husband a few weeks later. The lodger said, 'Don't laugh, but there's something not right in my room—it's been going on for about nine weeks now. Someone comes in during the night. I hear footsteps and heavy breathing, but when I switch on the light there is nothing there. Last night these noises woke me again, and half-asleep I called out, "Go away, I want to sleep." Then I was conscious of some power and felt a sharp pain in the lobe of my ear. Fully awake now, I got out of bed, put on the light and looked in the mirror. There was blood streaming down my neck from a gash in my ear. On the table beside the bed was a pair of nail scissors which I had put on the dressing table the night before, and there was fresh blood on the blades.'

In a very short while, although they had been there only just over two years, the Harrises put the house up for sale, but whereas most people in that situation scurry round with paintbrushes to make the place look more attractive, they brought in the Church to hold a service of exorcism. For eight hours two Anglican clergymen went from room to room, and in the eight weeks before they moved out, the family heard nothing more. But most interesting was the behaviour of the family pets, who had obviously been most unhappy in the house, moping and sidling reluctantly when they had to move from room to room. The moment the exorcism had ended they raced up and down the three floors, extremely excited and showing a playfulness they had not shown once in the previous two years.

Name supplied, Coventry

Aftermath of Murder

It is possible that some psychic phenomena can only be observed by those with a special sensitivity. It may be that there are people whose mental make-up is capable of receiving psychic 'broadcasts', and this could be the answer to a series of frightening events which took place in a three-storey Victorian house in West Bromwich high street in 1939.

The Stephensons, who occupied the whole house apart from a lock-up baker's shop on the ground floor, were a typical family, consisting of Mr Stephenson, who had a good job at a large glass works at Smethwick, Mrs Stephenson, and their two daughters, Irene (13) and Gladys (15). Irene, now a PhD describes the terrifying experiences she and her sister went through at intervals for almost two years:

> My sister and I shared a room on the top floor of this old, large house. At intervals of about three months we would be disturbed from our sleep at about 10pm by the sound of a woman's voice crying in distress. It came from the area of the bathroom on the second floor, on the opposite side of the house from our bedroom. The ghostly voice would start with a low moan, and then repeat what we thought was the name 'Duncan... Duncan...' As this went on it rose terrifyingly in pitch and intensity until it was an agonising scream, which cut off with chilling suddenness at its peak, leaving the air tingling in leaden silence with the imagined echoes of the awful sound. A few seconds later pandemonium would break loose as the whole house vibrated with what seemed to be six or seven people pounding in panic up and down the staircases and past our bedroom door. Once we dashed out, terrified, to see who was there, but although the mad stampede rushed past within a few feet of us, there was no one to be seen. We screamed at this ultimate in fear, and our parents, who in those pre-television days had been sitting in the ground floor sitting room listening to the radio, dashed up to us. They tried to reassure us that we had been dreaming, and that there had been nothing—but in later years my mother told me that they too had heard those ghastly sounds, but had denied it for fear of alarming

us any more. From time to time a different phenomena occurred—less noisy, but perhaps even more sinister in its obvious attempts at stealthy silence. My sister and I would be asleep when we were wakened by the sound of the door handle being rattled softly: the door seemed to open quietly, and someone entered—we could hear their clothes brushing against the wall as they surreptitiously sidled in, filled with menace. Perhaps, though, with the hindsight of age and experience, the sense of evil was subjective, the product of the instinctive dread of the unknown. But at the time, as the stealthy footsteps crossed to the bed, there was nothing but the overpowering feeling of malignancy. Then something sat on the edge of the bed, making the mattress sink as if a corporeal body were there: the light from the street lamp outside lit up the room so that we could see that there was no one there. Instinctively we huddled under the bedclothes, and though we could see nothing in the darkness, we knew that the presence had followed up, sometimes blowing cold air on our faces, sometimes touching them with icy fingers.

Not surprisingly, tensions mounted, culminating in the day when Mrs Stephenson, a strong-minded, practical woman, began spring cleaning in the small guest room on the top floor. She had dusted two drawers in a chest mechanically and without any conscious thought when, on opening the third she saw a small vest—the only garment in it—gyrating and dancing in an animated fashion. When the initial shock had subsided, she assumed that a mouse had got inside it, perhaps to make a nest, and had been disturbed. She picked up the article, shook it vigorously, found it empty, and then extremely puzzled, put it back where she had found it. To her utter horror it immediately began its frenzied and frantic writhing again: Mrs Stephenson's nerve broke, and slamming the drawer shut she bolted from the room. The family decided that they could take no more, and even though it meant giving up a good post, they decided to move back to their old home in Plymouth just before the war.

Shortly before leaving West Bromwich Irene was talking to a neighbour who, completely ignorant of anything that had happened in the house recently, mentioned casually that some years earlier a man had killed his niece in the bathroom. Irene still said nothing of the experiences the family had undergone, but in her mind she suddenly realised with a shudder that the cry 'Duncan... Duncan...' she had heard so many times could well, in the distortion and anguish of the situation, have been 'Uncle... Uncle...'

Mrs Irene Horner, Plymouth

The Five-year Phantom

One of the most frightening and yet at the same time most moving and pathetic of supernatural experiences associated with furniture centred itself on the Worthington family of Bradwell Road, Buckhurst Hill in the 1960s, and worked itself out not on a magnificent four-poster with centuries of history behind it, but an ordinary, prosaic modern wardrobe, made probably in the 1930s.

The Worthingtons married in 1956, and when James started his National Service a few weeks later Mary began to get a home together —no easy task, for even ten years after the end of the war many durables were still in short supply, or else shoddy or expensive. Reluctant to take on hire purchase commitments, Mary was delighted when her mother-in-law told her of a niece who was emigrating, and who was selling her furniture. Mary went to the address and bought on the spot a wardrobe, a dressing table and a chair.

The Worthingtons were delighted with their bargain, and over the next few years the home and future began to take shape: the first baby, John, was born in 1957; James returned to civilian life in 1958; Carol appeared in 1960 and her sister Lesley two years later. So far there had been little to distinguish the Worthingtons from thousands of other young families in the post-war years: their hopes and fears, like those of most other people, were based in the health and welfare of their children, in their home, and in the rising material prosperity. Then in 1962, when John was about five years old, a disturbing and indefinable element crept into the house in Bradwell Road. The main bedroom, in spite of Mary's efforts to air it, was permeated with a strong odour as if cosmetics had been spilt. No specific perfume was identifiable but it was, as she says, the sort of smell one found near the beauty counters at the large stores. At the same time young John often complained of someone coming into his room at night, but although the reports were frequent and consistent, his parents understandably attributed them to dreams and nightmares.

Less explicable were the sudden and mysterious disappearances from the bedroom of a number of articles. Especially strange was a pink cup which vanished without a trace and then several weeks later reappeared in a very conspicuous spot where it could not possibly have been overlooked and where it was impossible for a five-year-old to reach. Then as suddenly as they had begun, the smells, the nightmares and the disappearances ceased after a few months, and the whole episode was put down to 'one of those odd things'—that is, until 1965, when Carol was nearing her fifth birthday. Once again the pervasive

'She said a "little lady" had been standing on the landing "with a light shining round her".'

perfume filled the bedroom: again articles unaccountably disappeared, only to turn up in ridiculous and unexpected places. On one occasion Mary woke up to find that during the night a drawer from a small bedside table had projected itself across the room and lay on the floor on the opposite side.

When the second round of disturbances began to fade away some months later the Worthingtons suspected with dismay that they might in some way be connected with their children's age, so that in 1967 when Lesley approached five, tension began to grow. And once again, for several months the pointless perfume and the meaningless transportation of mundane articles repeated themselves. For Mary, who now had a fourth child, Nigel, this was the end, and for most of the time that her husband was away at work she wandered out of the house —anywhere to be free of whatever was lurking there, waiting for the next fifth birthday. Fortunately, not long afterwards, a brand new house became available some miles away and in fresh surroundings and in a bright, airy home never before occupied the fears of the past seemed to be little more than a half-forgotten nightmare.

Yet three years later as Nigel began to grow excited about his fifth birthday, the whole frightening cycle began its ominous round again. Only, as if something was aware that as far as the Worthingtons were concerned, this was a swan song, it reached a crescendo of terror. A fortnight after the first faint hints of the scented overture began to infiltrate the bedroom, ten-year-old Lesley suddenly screamed uncontrollably in the middle of the night, and when her father reached her she sobbed that 'a little lady' had been standing on the landing 'with a light shining round her'. When she had shouted, she said, the figure had gone down the stairs. As Lesley became pacified, she refused to accept the obvious solution of a dream: it was real, she insisted; she had seen it.

Exactly a week later, with all the other manifestations again in full swing, Mary lay sleepless in the early hours of the morning when to her extreme terror she saw a small girl emerge by the wardrobe round the bedroom door. Mary's screams tore her husband from sleep, but before he was fully conscious, the little figure had disappeared. It was only then that she recalled what the lady who had sold her the wardrobe had said as they chatted inconsequentially after the bargain had been struck—how the loss of her first child had brought her and her husband very close together. In the excitement of her purchase Mary had not thought the point worth mentioning, and she had not consciously recalled it for over sixteen years—until that moment. Now she knew the connection, and when she told James, he realised that they must now try to find out the truth.

The following morning they visited James' mother to see if she could add anything to the single fact they already knew. The story she told them—that the niece's daughter had died of cancer at the age of five—struck them with almost a physical blow. Mary knew that she could not stay another night in the house with the wardrobe that had seen, and brought, so much anguish. Newly married neighbours who knew nothing of its antecedents were delighted to have it as a gift, and although Mary felt a deep sense of guilt her doctor assured her that the experiences were entirely personal. For anyone else, he said, the wardrobe would be the harmless construction of wood and metal that it purported to be. Nevertheless, three days later as the neighbour was talking to Mary in the garden, she stopped mid-sentence, and rather frightened, said 'If I didn't know the house was empty, I could swear that someone was looking at me from the front bedroom window.' Two days later she appeared again in the garden, and extremely upset told Mary that during the darkness she had felt someone outside the bed gently grasp her hand. Terrified, she moved to another room and refused to enter the one in which the wardrobe had been placed, though at the time she did not connect it with her experiences.

Shortly after the neighbour left the district the wardrobe was destroyed. Since then, Mary says, her house has been completely happy and spirit free—though twice, she adds, she has smelt the faintest touch of the perfume, and on each occasion she has been told within twenty-four hours of the death of friends.

Name supplied, Essex

The Lonely Hunchback

There does not seem to have been, at least on the surface, any great trauma in the life of an old lady who lived in a cottage at Westbury-sub-Mendip, near Wells, yet her apparition seems to have appeared there almost nightly for a period of over six months in 1966.

In December 1965 Mrs Eileen Toomey went to join her husband who had taken a job on a farm at Westbury-sub-Mendip, and who was living at Stonleigh Cottages, a pair of agricultural houses probably built in the early nineteenth century but recently modernised with indoor sanitation to replace the traditional outside closet. At the front of the houses a garden wall blocked much of the view from the downstairs rooms, but from the bedroom window one could see straight along the lane to the traffic on the busy Wells to Cheddar road.

Soon after 10.30 as she lay in bed on her first night in the cottage, Eileen Toomey heard the back door rattling, and assuming it had been left

unfastened and was swinging in the wind, she switched on the light and went down to lock it. Moving quietly to avoid waking her two-month-old baby who was asleep in the cot by the window, she crept downstairs only to find the door shut, locked and without any movement that could have caused the noise. A little puzzled, she went back to bed making a mental note to see if there was anything outside that might have caused the sounds. A search in the morning revealed nothing, and the matter was dismissed—until about 10.30 the following night when the now-definite clicking of the latch and the shaking of the door began again. Once again Eileen inspected it, but there was nothing about the door, or in the dining room, that could possibly have been responsible.

After getting out of bed for five nights in a row only to find the downstairs silent and motionless when she reached it, Eileen decided that some oddity in the building itself must be responsible, and that however annoying and disturbing the noises might be she must put up with them for their brief, but mysteriously regular performance. And having made this decision the following night she did not switch on the light but lay awake in the darkness, slightly tensed, as ten-thirty approached.

Then, as on the previous nights, came the rattling from below. It died away, and in the taut silence that followed Eileen heard something she had not noticed before—the sound of quiet footsteps on the stairs. She turned round in bed automatically to face the door, but was shocked to disbelief when an elderly woman with a pronounced stoop and a longish skirt crossed the room to the window, where she stood silent and still, apparently bending at the end of the cot. From the first instant of its appearance there was no doubt about the phantom nature of the figure, for it was, Eileen says, all in reverse, like the negative of a black and white photograph: the light flesh tones of the face and hands were black, and the skirt a dusky grey. Eileen does not know how long the apparition remained because in sheer terror she hid under the blankets, and when at length she peered out, the room was in the normal darkness of midwinter with the cot vaguely silhouetted against the slightly less opaque blackness outside.

Some days later the neighbour asked across the garden if Eileen was settling in all right: she replied that apart from the ghost she was comfortable enough. The neighbour seemed very surprised and asked what had happened, but could offer no explanation. Some days later, however, the two women met again, and the neighbour revealed that the corporate village memory had thrown up some disturbing

'She stood silent and still at the window looking like the negative of a black and white photo.'

The home of 'the lonely hunchback'.

information. Some years earlier, it seemed, the cottage had been
occupied by a middle-aged farm worker whose wife had a deformity
which gave her a hunchbacked appearance. Probably because of this
she tended to spend most of her time indoors, sitting at the side of the
front bedroom window where she could see people moving freely about
the world. Her husband normally went to bed early because of his work,
but she did not usually follow until about 10.30, invariably making the
inconvenient but essential journey to the outside lavatory before she
did so. One morning her husband woke up to find his wife absent, and
her place obviously not slept in. Alarmed, he hurried downstairs and
found her lying dead in the outside closet, where she had collapsed and
died the previous night.

Although the story was frightening enough, it was a relief to Eileen:
she knew now that what she had thought was an ominous figure
crouching over her baby was the result of the poor woman's deformity,

and that far from being filled with malevolence and perhaps possessiveness, she was, pathetically, only returning to the one place where she could spend her passing time feeling secure and at peace.

Eileen Toomey says that until she left Stonleigh Cottages in May 1966, the apparition was almost a nightly visitor, and although the instinctive apprehension of the supernatural never completely left her, there was no longer the initial paralysing dread: indeed, she grew to feel that she could not go to sleep until the old lady, still in negative form, had come in and crossed to the window to see who knows what people and traffic hurry along the road, even though it was deserted and obscured by night.

Mrs Eileen Alford, Devon

The Ouija Board Woman

It is surprising how often letters received when compiling this book referred to the ouija board—strangely enough generally as a side issue or explanation of an apparition rather than in the more usual context of communicating with 'the spirits'. Several correspondents mention the appearance of an apparition to someone not connected with the 'seance', which is often being conducted in a half-serious way by adolescents in another part of the building, or even in a nearby house, and quite unknown to the actual witness. One of the best-described incidents of this unusual manifestation comes from Fraserburgh in Scotland.

Thirty-three-year-old Robert Cowe had just returned home from the Merchant Navy in 1973. He was, he says, in excellent spirits, with no worries, no strain and was delighted to relax in his parents' flat at 12 High Street—a building erected about 1820. After coffee he went to bed, slept soundly, but woke about 2.30am with that intense craving for a cigarette that comes with such overpowering strength when you know you have none. The awful struggle between lying tormented by longing in the warmth and comfort of bed, and the cold uncomfortable journey downstairs and out into the night to the vending machine some 55 yards away, raged in his mind for some minutes until he was cruelly wide awake and acutely conscious of his dilemma.

Gradually, as the cosiness of the blankets began to retreat in the face of the nicotine forces, Robert sat up in bed and immediately became

(Overleaf) 'The figure gradually took shape into the features of an elderly woman who seemed to be trying to say something.'

aware of a vague and unrecognisable presence in the room. But before he could really start logically to analyse what he thought it might be, a figure started to form, rather like those titles in some animated films that build themselves into recognisable words from a random mass of dots and lines. The most clearly defined areas at the beginning were near the floor, where Robert to his complete incredulity could make out distinctly black shoes with large silver buckles, and black stockings. Gradually a blue and white check dress and a white apron settled out, and finally the head and features of an elderly woman with gingery hair drawn to the back of her head, apparently into a bun, though this was not visible.

The figure, now sharp and clear in its entirety, stood about a yard from the bed, stooping and leaning forward. The woman, aged between 60 and 70, looked intently at Robert and seemed to be fighting to say something but was unable to do so. The impression that the apparition had something to communicate became so intense that Robert mumbled, 'What do you want?' This seemed only to increase the figure's frustration and anxiety, and it leaned further forward though not over the bed. But as still no sound emerged, Robert repeated his question, and then, thoroughly scared, he shouted, '*What do you want?*'

Immediately a remarkable change came over the phantom. Robert describes it: 'Still keeping its outline the apparition began to glow in what seemed tiny particles of electrified dust—and then disappeared completely. The room felt intensely cold . . .' He leaped from bed to switch on the light, but as he had expected, there was absolutely nothing that could have accounted for what he had seen.

Nothing Robert could remember in his own life seemed to have led to the haunting, and certainly it does not seem to have been the herald of any great change. He did discover later, however, that Gina Wiseman, the owner of the building, and some young friends had been holding a ouija board session on that night in the flat above, and without any prompting she told him that they had contacted a lady who had lived in the house a century earlier. The two incidents may, of course, have been nothing more than coincidence, but when several similar experiences are recorded from different parts of the country, it does make one hesitate to dismiss the relationship out of hand.

Robert Cowe, Fraserburgh

'It's Tannahill Again'

The strange happenings at James A Stewart's clothing mill at Dunmurry, near Belfast tell the story of a kindly ghost—the ghost of a man whose dedication and responsibility to his job survived even his death.

The clothing mill is typical of the stark, red-brick architecture of the 1870s, unlovely to any but the most ardent Victoriana-phile, yet the spirit of the place seems to have meant a great deal to a most unlikely character, William Tannahill, the caretaker and night watchman. Billy may have had a reputation of not looking too closely for extra jobs about the place, even though it was generally admitted that he did his prescribed duties most conscientiously, but he seems to have felt more deeply about his nightly patrols of the deserted building than anyone realised. All that was known was that as regularly as the clock itself he stumped from his tiny company cottage attached to the factory, through the lofty, empty rooms and passages, past the silent machinery at 10.30pm, at 3.0am and again at 6.0am, when he opened up the boilers for the day's work.

In 1963 Billy died, and Albert, a company pensioner, agreed to do his job until a permanent replacement could be found. It was during Albert's short incumbency, a few days after Tannahill's death, that Mr N I Irwin, undermanager at the factory, let himself and a friend into his office about ten-thirty one evening to collect some papers he had forgotten. Hearing the night watchman's footsteps patrolling overhead and not wishing to alarm the old man, he called out, 'It's all right, Bertie, it's only me—Ian.' There was no reply and the footsteps ceased. Believing he had surprised an intruder, Mr Irwin dashed upstairs to the room immediately overhead leaving his friend to guard the narrow stairs.

The room at the top was empty: a search of the large cupboards in it revealed nothing, and the two men were about to move on to search the rest of the upper floor when they realised that the only other door leading from the room was locked on the inside, so that no one could have left without passing them. Although inwardly unconvinced, they tacitly agreed that they must have been imagining the footsteps.

Three days later a new night watchman, Hugh, was appointed on a three-week probationary period but moved immediately into Tannahill's vacant cottage. With the security of the factory now more or less settled, Mr Irwin might well have forgotten the mysterious incident of the previous week, had not the general manager one morning casually reported that he had been in the works late the evening before and hearing the watchman's footsteps moving round the upper floor had called out to reassure him. Like Irwin, he had received no response, and after a long search through the building had found no trace of anyone or of anything disturbed. The two men agreed that coincidence was now being stretched too far and that the incidents must be kept quiet for fear of alarming the staff, particularly as there was the possibility of night shifts.

But the phantom prowler was not to be so easily hushed up: the following week the maintenance engineer reported agitatedly that he and another mechanic had been working late on a faulty boiler the previous evening and had heard heavy footsteps on the upper floor. As Hugh the new night watchman was with them in the boiler room it was obvious that there was an intruder, and the three men went through the whole factory thoroughly. Like the others, they found no one, nor any sign of entry or damage. Two days before the end of Hugh's probationary period the night watchman met Mr Irwin in a corridor and as casually as if he were reporting a broken light bulb, said, 'It's Tannahill—we have him in the cottage. We hear his footsteps going down the stairs about 10.20 every evening; the front door seems to open and close, and then he comes back about 11. His footsteps go upstairs again, and his bedroom door closes. It's all quiet then until just after two in the morning, and then again about half past five, when the whole performance goes on again.' Hugh was not in the least disturbed: he said that Tannahill did no damage and upset no one, least of all himself.

In the three weeks following Bill's death about thirty people claimed to have heard not only the plodding footsteps but also the opening and closing of doors he had used on his rounds, though those which had been propped open or not used remained obstinately silent. At the end of the month Hugh was confirmed in his post: three days later he met Mr Irwin again and said in his usual deadpan tones: 'Do you want something for the records? It's Tannahill again. The day I got the letter appointing me to the job permanently, his footsteps stopped entirely in the cottage, and I suppose in the factory. I suppose Billy couldn't trust me until you were satisfied, and made his three rounds a night just to make sure for himself that everything was all right.' Certainly central heating pipes do not fall silent suddenly, but from the day of Hugh's appointment as official guardian of the building, the spectral steps were never reported again.

N I Irwin, Sussex

The Cold Staring Eyes

The hours of night have always been the traditional haunting time: darkness with its shadows and fears seems natural to the supernatural. But though many contemporary psychic phenomena are still experienced at night, a surprising number occur in broad daylight, often in the most prosaic circumstances. What more unlikely situation for an apparition can there be than a Sunday afternoon family drive in the car.

In mid-November 1968, a rather dull heavy day, Olive Bryant and her husband were returning to their home in Worcester after a Sunday jaunt to Gloucester, and as Mr Bryant was particularly interested in church architecture they decided to turn off the main A38 road towards Deerhurst Priory. The narrow lane ended at the gate of the churchyard, and Olive waited in the car outside with the dog while her husband clambered over the stile to take the gravel path towards the church itself.

As she sat there waiting, the grey afternoon seemed to settle down more oppressively than before so that the possibility of anyone else coming to the lonely spot was remote. However, after a short while a young man with a red face came down the path from the church, leaned on the gate staring vacantly for a few minutes and then returned the way he had come. Some minutes later the vicar, humming to himself and carrying a rolled umbrella walked up the lane from behind the car, padlocked the churchyard gate and then, climbing over the stile, walked towards the church. Both incidents were so trivial that had there been any other activity it is unlikely that they would have registered at all with Mrs Bryant: as it was, she recalls every detail.

After this flurry the silence, the oppressiveness, and the loneliness closed about the place more stiflingly. Olive grew fidgety at her husband's unexpectedly long absence. Then, from the direction of a black and white timbered building beyond the churchyard there came the whining of a dog. She glanced round and to her surprise—as no one had passed the car or come from the church—she saw an elderly woman, about a dozen yards away dressed incongruously in clothes the fashion of about forty years earlier. As she remained in sight for at least a quarter of an hour altogether, Olive could note her appearance in minute detail: the cloche hat; the broad-collared, mid-thigh-length green coat; the black shoes; the open-back gloves, and the lisle stockings. Olive knew that fashions in the country tend to lag a little behind those of the cities, but no one but an eccentric would be almost half a century out of date. And the woman's behaviour seemed to confirm that she was a little unbalanced: she stared straight at Mrs Bryant in a most aggressive way without moving.

After a few minutes of this intense scrutiny Olive felt embarrassed by the hard, unblinking stare, and began quite unnecessarily to tidy the floor and glove box of the car to relieve the tension. All the while the dog, who had leaped into the back, kept up a frightened growling in his throat and refused to be pacified. When she thought the unpleasant woman might have gone, Olive glanced up, but the strange character was still there, gazing as before. Olive flinched, looked aside momentarily through the side window, and then back again. And in that second the woman had moved until she was standing right up against the radiator of the car. It would have been impossible for anyone to have covered the distance in the brief instant she had been out of vision, but it still did not enter Olive's head that the figure was anything other than that of a mentally disturbed local.

From her nearer and more threatening position the woman continued her unwavering and hostile stare until some minutes later a small yellow car approached along the lane. As it stopped the figure turned quickly, mounted the stile and began to walk towards the church. A woman with a bundle of music—presumably the organist coming to arrange for the evening service—emerged from the yellow car and without a glance at Mrs Bryant hurried a few yards behind the green-coated lady towards the church. After a few steps both were hidden by the tall, dense hedge.

Almost immediately, and certainly before either of the two women could have reached the church building, Mr Bryant climbed back over the stile, looking a little disturbed. 'Let's get away from here,' he said as he got into the car. 'You could cut the atmosphere in the church with a knife.' When Olive remarked that with characters like the one who had just gone up the path she was not surprised, her husband asked if she meant the organist. Olive said that she meant the strange lady with the old-fashioned clothes who was just ahead of the lady with the music. Her husband stared blankly: he was adamant that there had been only one person, and there was certainly nowhere anyone could have hidden. Olive was equally certain there had been two, only a few paces apart, and that it would have been impossible to pass one without seeing the other. And for the first time the possibility that the figure might have been an apparition began to dawn. The Bryants drove home in silence, their emotions—bewilderment, annoyance, despair or fear—concealed in incomprehension.

And incomprehensible the affair remained: in retrospect Olive has tried to establish a link between the strange phantom and a series of personal tragedies that fell on her five years later, but any such association seems to stretch coincidence and imagination impossibly.

Mrs Olive Bryant, Yorkshire

Servant in the Shadows

Perhaps the most frustrating of apparitions are those which are so clear and so definite, and although described in detail by several witnesses, cannot be associated with any specific person or event. In 1956 William Horner, a 17-year-old apprentice joiner, together with his journeyman, Joe Robinson, had been working for a month on maintenance in the rambling 50-room mansion on the Cairnsmore estate, some eight miles from Newton Stewart. The house could have been designed as a setting for a classic horror film. Set in wild countryside with a backdrop of grey hills, it had not been lived in for many years, although it was kept fully furnished in an earlier style. Translated into human terms, it was in a kind of suspended animation, a living dead. And as if to emphasise this, mains electricity had not yet marched over the moor on its pylon legs, but the house had a supply of a kind from a venerable and temperamental generator which gave illumination a little more convenient, if not a great deal brighter, than candles and oil lamps.

So it was with some relief that the two men packed their tools about 3.30 on a November afternoon on the last day of their work. They had just loaded their equipment into the van outside, and were returning to the house for a final check, when they were stopped dead in their tracks in the great entrance hall by the first sounds they had heard in the building apart from those they had made themselves. It was a most unusual rising and falling rumble, beating rhythmically from the ceiling of the ground floor. The immediate reaction of the two men was that one of the bedroom ceilings was collapsing in a rain of plaster, but the next moment, to their relief, they recognised it as the sound of the huge, antique, hand-propelled carpet sweeper that was kept at the end of the first floor corridor. If pushed with sufficient power the cumbersome machine both swept and beat the carpet with a characteristic thudding —the two men had been so intrigued by the apparatus that early in their visit they had tried it out to see how it worked.

For the moment the mystery was cleared up: it seemed rational that someone should be cleaning up behind them now that their work had finished, but almost before the idea had really formed they knew that that explanation was impossible. No one else had been to the house all the time they had been working there, and it seemed most unlikely that anyone should do so then. In any case, a visitor would have had to pass the two men to enter the building, and certainly no one had done so. So, they were brought back to their original idea of a collapsing ceiling, and dashed up the main staircase to the first floor corridor from which the family and guest bedrooms opened off. As they reached the head of the stairs, the carpet sweeping sound ceased abruptly, and as they searched every room they found that not a speck of the very-evident dust had stirred. Reaching the end of the corridor in their search, they turned, non-plussed, because although there was the servants' floor above them, the noises had definitely come from the level on which they were standing.

Then suddenly, as they stood discussing the next move, a woman emerged from an open bedroom door halfway along the corridor, and without glancing in their direction walked away from them towards a flight of spiral stairs that led upwards to the second floor and attics. She wore a long, dark dress that suggested a fashion of some fifty years earlier, and her hair was swept up and piled on top of her head. These details, and the fact that the position of the arms suggested that she was carrying something in front of her, made a very deep impression on William Horner.

It did not dawn on them at that moment that her odd clothing, her utter silence, her strange behaviour in not acknowledging their presence, and the sheer impossibility of her being there at all, precluded a living human being. It was only when on reaching the foot of the staircase that she hesitated for an instant, and then immediately vanished, that the first suspicions and dread began to crystallise. But even then they clung to the frail hope that it was a joke, played in a way they could not comprehend. The figure had definitely not gone to the second floor the stairs had been in full view all the time, even though the lighting was not particularly bright, but as the men knew that this part of the house would have to be checked before they left, they went up together, rather reluctantly.

At the top they pressed the switch which illuminated the upper corridor, and as the generator laboured with the additional load, a red-tinged glow lit the passage from end to end. There some twelve yards away, stood the woman they had seen on the floor beneath, motionless, but with the same long dark dress and the upswept hair, looking straight at them—at least, there was the impression of staring, though in the grey shadow that served as a face there were no distinguishable features. For two endless seconds the two men watched, frozen, and then simultaneously with limbs loosened, they bolted down two flights to the open air. They knew that no living person could have passed them to reach the top storey; they knew that the windows opened sheer to the ground forty feet below—and yet she was there.

With the hair on their necks bristling they dashed to the caretaker in his lodge, leaving the lights burning in the house with reckless prodigality. The old man, a retired gamekeeper from the estate, was, William Horner says, the stereotype dour Scot: had a ghostly Bonnie Prince Charlie and a phantom army marched down the drive he

'She stood twelve yards away staring at them from a featureless, shadowy face.'

probably would, without a flicker of feeling, have merely said that the master was not at home. Now, with as little emotion as if he were explaining a drain blocked by falling leaves, or a damp patch caused by a fallen tile, he rationalised the figure. A suicide, maybe, or more likely the tradition of the maid who had been killed in the late nineteenth century when the pony and trap she was driving crashed through the parapet of the bridge into the river running through the estate.

But whatever the explanation—if indeed there was one, or needs to be one—it does not concern William Horner, who says that even today he feels that intense prickling of terror as the clarity and detail of the ghostly woman returns to him—as it so often does.

William Horner, Glasgow

The Unpredictable Apparition

A strange female spirit has appeared to three different people between 1969 and 1971 at an old farmhouse in south Hampshire, a building of great age, standing on a site which has had human habitation for perhaps thousands of years.

Claverton Farm, between Winchester and Bishops Waltham stands on a site where there is a continuous record of a dwelling for over 800 years. Less than a hundred yards away are traces of Roman settlements, perhaps from the first century of our era. It is not only its age that is remarkable, but also its standing: as early as the thirteenth century when the majority of peasants were tied to the manor or the church by feudal bonds of service, the Claverton family were living on the farm as free tenants, paying to the Abbot of Tichfield a nominal rent of half a pound of cumin seed a year. This freedom was achieved usually by faithful or notable service to the feudal lord, and as well as being excused the humiliating duties of serfdom, gained the tenant the title of Franklin. By the Tudor period their average holding was about 150 acres, making them a kind of rustic middle-class with some of the material prosperity but none of the social standing, of the gentry. Unfortunately, though the Claverton family farmed the land for over 350 years they produced very little in the way of permanent record. An occasional glimpse of the succession glimmers through the dust of an

'Don't tell me: let me tell you. I have just seen a woman wearing a cloak and hood. She moved behind me and went out through the door.'

old legal document, but it is generally information about the property rather than the people.

By 1930 the farm had fallen low in its fortunes: the land was sour and unproductive; the woods were overgrown and neglected and the house itself had been split into two cottages for farm workers. During the war the land was reclaimed and became very productive with the farm buildings occupied by prisoners of war. But by 1945 the house was empty and derelict again. Standing half a mile from the nearest road and neighbour, without water, sanitation or electricity it was left to moulder under creeping brambles, ivy, elder and wild thyme.

It was at this time that the present owners discovered it and recognised the peace and beauty of the place, just as some invading Saxon had 1500 years earlier. As far as possible without altering the basic structure and character of the house they restored it until it offered twentieth-century standards of comfort comparable to those enjoyed by the Clavertons at the height of their prosperity in the sixteenth century.

In 1969, soon after the alterations had been completed, the wife of the present owner was sleeping alone in the house. Suddenly, and for no apparent reason she found herself wide awake. Opening her eyes she became aware of a figure standing at the foot of the bed. The body was vague and appeared to be wearing a cloak with a hood, but the face stood out in natural colour with extraordinary clarity. It was of a youngish woman, who seemed to radiate an immense peace. The lady of the house noted the hazel eyes, and the sweet, kindly expression. She and the apparition smiled at each other, and then without any trace of disquiet, she turned over and went straight back to sleep. She mentioned the incident to her husband when he returned, but didn't refer to it again until the following year when an ex-naval Petty Officer called at the farm on business. For some time he and the owner sat discussing prosaic mechanical matters. The host then moved to the corner of the room to refill their glasses and, when he returned to his chair was immediately asked, 'Is this house haunted?' A little startled, the owner hesitated, and the sailor interjected with, 'No—don't tell me: let me tell you. I have just seen a woman wearing a cloak and hood. She moved behind me and went out through that door.' Once again, there was absolutely no feeling of distress or alarm, only, the visitor said, an atmosphere of great tranquility.

The third appearance was more sinister. In 1971 two old friends of the owners, on leave from Hong Kong, were staying on the farm overnight. The wife was an exceptionally beautiful woman, and after an evening of reminiscing in front of the log fire, the guests retired to bed. In the early hours of the morning the wife awoke in great distress, crying out, 'No! No! She is trying to get inside my body. She wants my body!' Her husband soothed her by saying that it had been a nightmare, and after a while the wife became composed, and went back to sleep.

It was not until nearly two years later that the husband returned to the farm on his own: only then did he tell the owners of the terrifying nightmare his wife had experienced there, and, unaware of the previous incidents, said that his wife had told him the phantom in her dream who had desired to possess her body had been a beautiful woman in her early thirties—a description which seemed to tally uncannily with those of the two other witnesses.

Since then many visitors of all ages have stayed at the farm, but none has reported anything out of the normal, which makes this weird haunting all the more puzzling. Of all the hundreds of people who had lived out their lives in this hollow in the downs, few have left any record other than a name. But perhaps among them somewhere is one— repressed, guilty, remorseful, jealous or ecstatically happy—who cannot rest. But why should she appear in this strange form? Did she appear after the changes in the building to show her approval or disapproval? Have the three appearances completed the cycle or does the face wait for a propitious moment or suitable person to manifest itself once more? Perhaps the most intriguing mystery is the change of attitude: does this imply nothing more than the subjective response of the three observers to the apparition, or more frighteningly, does it mean a conscious reaction on the part of the ghost to the individuals concerned? Or did something happen in time between the second and third appearances to change the feelings of this strange restless spirit?

Name supplied, Hampshire

The Haunted Sick Bay

It has been suggested that the intense emotions which surround birth and death are responsible for the considerable number of supernatural experiences in hospitals and with medical staff, but it is not always these most profound of feelings that are the cause. Probably no patient ever died in the RAF sick quarters at Bletchley, and few were seriously ill, yet this was the scene of a well-authenticated haunting. Rev John Storey, now a Unitarian minister in Lincoln writes:

From October 1953 to March 1956 I served at RAF Bletchley as a medical orderly. The patients were generally in their teens, suffering from minor complaints, more serious illnesses being sent to a larger

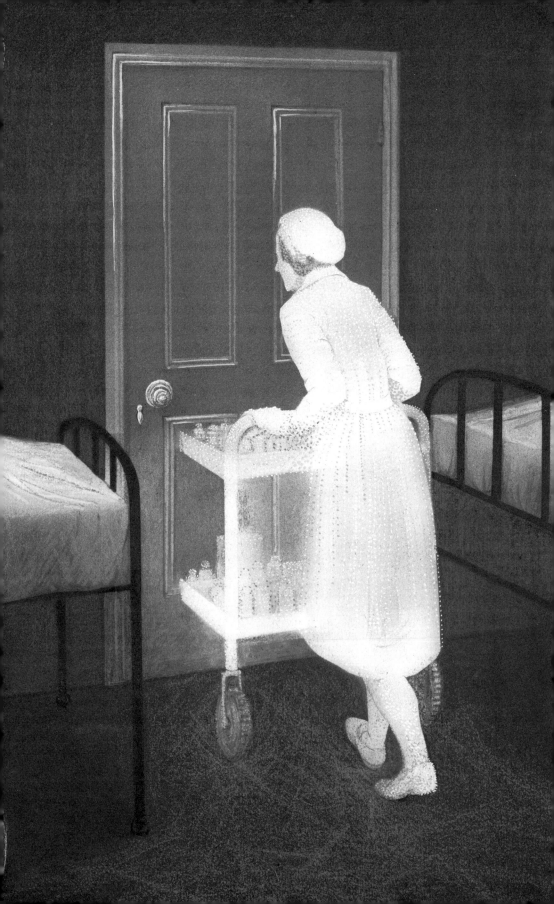

hospital. During my two-and-a-half years in the sick quarters a number of patients reported independently seeing a woman pushing a trolley through the ward during the hours of darkness. One patient described her as wearing a green apron. All reports agreed that she disappeared through a door at the end of the ward. In my time this door led to an open space but I believe that at one time there had been another room beyond it. I never saw the apparition myself, but oddly enough I once heard it. I was in the ward as a patient myself at the time, when a noise by the sink in the corner of the ward (it was only a small ward) woke me from a light sleep. I then heard the unmistakable sound of a trolley which I felt was carrying surgical instruments, being wheeled past the foot of my bed. But I saw nothing.

Mr Storey added that during the Second World War the station had been used by service personnel of both sexes, but that during most of his time there it was exclusively male. The apparition continued to be reported he said, but he believes the building is now demolished. One wonders whether this dedicated orderly still pushes her trolley over the waste ground—or whether this was an apparition only the sick could see.

Rev J A Storey, Lincoln

The Secret Garden

In November 1945 young Peter Turner and his friends were playing through the derelict maze of industrial revolution terraced houses that made up the Camp Hill area of Leeds. Many of the buildings had already been demolished, and most of the rest had been stripped, officially and unofficially, until only the shells remained to form a prohibited playground for the local children. There was not only the physical thrill and danger of scrambling through the crumbling skeletons, but also the excitement of avoiding authority as the tottery structures were under both public and parental interdictions. The particular row in which Peter and his friends were playing that afternoon had been stripped of floorboards, and as he jumped from rafter to rafter of the upper floor, he glanced through one of the window holes into the sea of rubble below. To his amazement there were no heaps of broken brick and mortar and shattered timber: instead he looked down

'She disappeared through a door at the end of the ward.' ·

into a well-kept garden about five yards by four, with rose trees in bloom and an elderly man tending them.

The utter impossibility of any garden, much less one with roses in full bloom in November being there at all did not strike him at the moment: uppermost in his mind was the fear of being caught for the double crime of trespass and disobedience, and shouting to his friends, he fled lest the man should catch him. It was only later that reality dawned. He searched, but the heaps of waste obstinately remained heaps of waste, and the few sparse annual weeds that had managed to grow refused to turn into bushes of roses. Today the spot is buried beneath the new Merrion Centre and Peter Turner occasionally wonders as he wanders round the shops exactly where the garden lies beneath the concrete and terazzo, and what trick of time or mind showed it to him.

The supernatural in Leeds had not yet finished with Peter Turner: in 1956, some six months before his marriage, he took the top flat at 10 Woodhouse Square, a tall Georgian house, now demolished. The rooms in which he lived had in the building's grander days been a fine nursery, but now it was in a sorry state of repair. So, in the months before his wedding, he worked hard redecorating and making the flat presentable, pressing any volunteer help he could get. He always felt that there was something strange about the place that he could not pinpoint precisely, but working all day as an engineer, and all the evening as a painter-decorator, it would have taken an army of phantoms to keep him from sleep.

One evening however, two lady friends of his mother were helping him with the painting, and at the end of the session Peter went with one of them to get fish and chips for supper, leaving the other to clear up. On their return they found their companion halfway down the stairs, terrified to go back into the flat because of the strange noises and sensations. But in the excitement of the wedding these oddities were pushed into the background.

The tensions of early days of marriage and the loneliness of the new housewife are said to cause many disturbances, but it did not seem to Pamela Turner that these factors could be responsible for the strange behaviour of some of the doors in the flat. From time to time the door of a large walk-in cupboard in the living room opened gently—no matter how securely it had been fastened—and what appeared to be the sound of footsteps crossed the room. The living room door itself would then click open, and all would be silent. On other occasions Pamela would be standing at the sink when the cupboard door swung ajar: she would

'Instead of rubble and junk he saw a beautiful garden, tended by an elderly man.'

154

hear the shuffling steps and then be conscious of an invisible presence standing immediately behind her.

The most frightening series of events occurred after one of Pamela's friends, who had been unable to come to the wedding, called, and asked if she could see the dress. This was brought out, admired, packed away again, and the friend left. The whole incident was so normal that it was scarcely noted, but that night, after the Turners had gone to bed, there were the unmistakable sounds of the bed-settee being dragged heavily across the floor of the living room. When Peter dashed in, nothing had moved even an inch.

The same sounds occurred again a few nights later, and then came the appalling crash as they recognised the heavy cast iron mangle being thrown over. The two previous incidents had told them that they would find the huge machine as upright and stable as ever when they rushed in, and so it was. This disturbance, however, was too much for the people in the flat below who complained bitterly about the Turners moving their furniture so noisily in the middle of the night. Soon after the Turners left 10 Woodhouse Square with deep relief, and for them in their new house all was quiet.

A most intriguing sequel was yet to come: some time later they attended an adult education centre in another house in the square, and met an elderly lady who in the course of conversation said that she had been brought up in number 10. It was reputed then, she told them, to be haunted by a young Victorian wife whose two children had died, and who searched for them constantly in the nursery. The old lady went on to say that when her family moved into the house in the last years of the nineteenth century, they found a number of boxes and trunks in the cellar. All were empty—except one, which contained a wedding dress.

Is it a coincidence that the new building on the site of the old number 10 is the office of the RSPCC?

Mrs Pamela Turner, Leeds

The Eye

It has been said before that the bizarre nature of many contemporary supernatural experiences gives them a unique air of authenticity: the filmy, translucent fancy dress figure at midnight could so easily be a mental regurgitation of a stock ghost story or TV play, and must, in the absence of any corroborative evidence be looked at very carefully. The

'She saw a pale blue human eye staring up at her from a knot hole in the floor.'

experiences of Mrs Violet Nicholls, of 18 Hall End Lane, Pattingham—a semi-detached house built about 1930—began in this almost stereotyped routine way, but soon developed into something much more extraordinary, almost, indeed, grotesque.

One night in 1952 Mrs Nicholls says that she woke up and saw standing in the bedroom a young woman in her mid-twenties, with a beautiful complexion, long blonde hair and a full-length yellow dress 'marked at the waist like a half moon'. Terrified of the stranger she woke up her husband who reluctantly searched the house: not finding anything he was very annoyed and returned to sleep. Violet, very disturbed, remained awake, and then in the darkness saw the bedroom door open. The same woman put her head in, looked round and apparently assured that all was right, vanished.

A week later about midday, Violet was alone in the house, and looking out of the kitchen window saw the same young lady, her hair swinging and her cheeks glowing, coming up the garden path. Extremely surprised, Violet saw the figure pass the kitchen door, and then vanish, disappearing forever from her life, unless, of course, the terrifying incident which occurred six years later is in some strange way connected with the lovely female phantom.

In 1958 Violet, then aged 40, was living on her own with her five-year-old son Christopher John. One evening as usual she sent him up to bed to undress, and then followed a few minutes later to tuck him in bed, only to find him staring with utter bewilderment at the floor near the fireplace. 'Look, mum,' he whispered in an awed voice, pointing to a large knot hole in one of the boards. Violet looked, not expecting anything but some trivial mark, and then, almost too astonished to believe her own senses saw a pale blue, but unmistakably human eye staring up at her. She and Christopher stood transfixed with fear and amazement as the eye, which at first seemed to be frightened and then cautiously watchful, glared unblinkingly upwards.

From time to time it moved up and down within the limits of the cavity beneath as if trying to escape: finally it drifted slowly to one side, but did not vanish out of sight until between five and ten minutes later when it faded away. Christopher, now married and with the scepticism of his twenties, confirms the story exactly, but can offer no explanation for the strange events of that evening, which have never in any way been repeated.

Mrs Violet Nicholls, Wolverhampton

Clarissa's Pig

Some of the great eastern religions believe that human beings can be reincarnated as animals as punishment for evil ways in this life, and although western creeds reject this idea of rebirth, the concept does find an echo in the common belief that some ghosts—particularly those of suicides—occasionally manifest themselves in the shape of a beast. An example of this type of haunting comes from Hoe Benham, near Newbury.

At the beginning of the century Laburnham Villa at Hoe Benham was owned by two young artists, Oswald Pittman and Reginald Waud, who on the morning of 2 November 1907 were painting in the garden studio while they awaited the arrival of a friend, Miss Clarissa Miles, who lived nearby. About 10am Pittman went up to the cottage to give the jug to the milkman who had just arrived and looking along the lane that led to the house saw Miss Miles approaching with easel and palette, and much to his surprise, accompanied by a very large white pig with an abnormally long snout. When told of the fact Waud rather tartly commented that he hoped Clarissa would leave her new friend outside and would close the gate securely as she knew very well the pride they took in the garden.

A few minutes later when Miss Miles arrived she was alone, and was rather taken aback when she heard what Pittman had seen, for she said, if she had not actually seen the creature she must have heard its grunting and pattering. She was, however, sufficiently disturbed to retrace her steps towards the village to search for the animal but found nothing: children who had been playing in the lane as she passed said they had seen no pig, and the following morning the milkman signed a statement that Miss Miles had certainly been alone when he saw her. It was not surprising that there were no animals loose as the whole area was under a swine fever order, and any straying livestock was liable to be destroyed.

Pittman and Waud left for London soon afterwards but returned in February to continue painting. It seems that up to this point there had been little contact between them and the villagers—as townees, artists and two young men living together they were bound to excite suspicion—but the tale of the phantom pig broke the reserve. They were inundated with accounts of earlier animal apparitions which it was believed locally stemmed from a farmer named Tommy King whose property had bordered the lane and who had committed suicide in one of the barns. The farm and its outbuilding had been demolished in 1892 when the land was sold. But though his home had vanished Tommy King still seemed to be very much in evidence. The parish registers record the deaths of two Tommy Kings, one in 1741 and the other in

1753, and it is not known which of them is responsible for the hauntings.

One elderly villager, John Barrett, told Pittman and Waud how as a lad in 1850 he had been returning with seven or eight men in a hay waggon along the lane when near King's Farm the horses suddenly went wild. Everyone in the waggon saw a white shape dancing above the horses' heads. 'This white thing kept a-bobbin' and a-bobbin', and the hosses kept a-snortin' and a-snortin'' until they reached a spot where two gates faced each other across the lane. Here the white shape floated into a field and vanished.

At the same spot in 1873 John Barrett saw in broad daylight a creature 'summat like a sheep' pawing the ground in the middle of the road. He hit at it with his stick, but the apparition disappeared before the blow reached it. Albert Thorne reported that in the autumn of 1904 he heard a buzzing noise like 'a whizzin' of leaves' and saw 'summat like a calf knuckled down'. The animal was about two and a half feet high and five feet long with glowing eyes, but though he kept his gaze on it, it gradually faded from sight. Another unnamed witness said that on a bright moonlit night in January 1905 he saw a large black animal which he assumed to be the curate's dog near the gates in the lane. He was about to grab it and return it to its owner when it seemed to turn into a black donkey which reared on its hind legs before vanishing.

With these stories fresh in their minds Pittman, Waud and Clarissa Miles decided to walk the length of the lane to the main A4 road after evensong to look more closely at the places mentioned. Although they probably did not expect to experience anything it was obvious as they passed the site of King's Farm that Miss Miles became extremely distressed. She said that she felt the overwhelming presence of an awful being charged with malice and evil towards them and at the same time a terrifying physical sensation of suffocation.

On their return they heard an 'unearthly scream' apparently from the middle of the track near Laburnham Villa, and white and silent they hurried back to the house. Once inside and secure, they discussed the frightening sound, which became even more terrifying when Pittman assured them that it had occurred exactly at the spot where he had seen the phantom pig.

Society for Psychical Research

'She seemed to be accompanied by a large, white pig.'

(Overleaf) They saw a white shape dancing over the horses' heads.

The Phantom Hitchhiker

The notorious A38, now happily replaced for much of its length by motorway, carves across England from Derby to Cornwall, cutting across Birmingham, Gloucester, Bristol, Taunton, Exeter and Plymouth on the way. In summer it was a road to make the veteran motorist blanch with terror—at the infamous bottlenecks and miles of motionless cars baked in the sun. But the A38 for a ten mile stretch centred on Wellington in Somerset has an evil reputation far removed from traffic jams—it seems to be the haunt of a phantom who, torch in hand, tries to flag down passing motorists at night. Although the tradition had been well established for a number of years, it was a report in the *Western Morning News* in August 1970 that brought stories flooding in.

A Mrs K Swithenbank, said the *News*, had been driving from the village of Oake to her home in Taunton late one evening when she saw what appeared to be a middle-aged man dressed in a long grey overcoat or mackintosh standing in the middle of the road near Heatherton Grange Hotel. His face was averted and he appeared to be holding a torch pointing to the ground. Mrs Swithenbank was confronted by the figure suddenly as she rounded a bend, and as there was no time to brake she swerved violently. There was no impact, and a moment later when she looked, the road was completely empty in both directions.

While a single instance might have been generally attributed to one of the scores of mental or physical factors that are the origin of so many apparitions, however sincerely reported, confirmation of the experience came rapidly. Two other motorists claimed that they too had seen an identical figure in the same place and had taken similar action, and a motor cyclist who had encountered what seems to have been the same phantom at White Ball, some four miles to the west, fell from his machine and broke a limb. Another motorist said that he had seen the figure at White Ball, but on this occasion it was looking along its shoulder so that its face, invisible in the majority of sightings, was clear in profile.

The publication of these reports led Mr Harold Unsworth, a long distance lorry driver of Exeter, to break a twelve-year silence—a silence he had kept partly for fear of ridicule, but more because he could scarcely bring himself to believe what he had seen. In a letter to the *Exeter Express and Echo* he described how he had been driving back to his depot at Cullompton at about 3am when he had been flagged down near the Blackbird Inn, about one mile west of Hatherton Grange, by a middle-aged man in a grey or cream mackintosh carrying a torch. The weather was foul, and the man, hatless, with curling grey hair hanging down almost to his collar, seemed to be so wet and

miserable that Mr Unsworth, despite the risk at that time of night on a lonely road, gave him a lift.

The man, who appeared by his speech to be well-educated, asked to be dropped about four miles along the road at the old Beam Bridge at Holcombe, and as they travelled he described with the most gruesome delight, the accidents that had happened at the bridge. Mr Unsworth was not sorry to get rid of his strange passenger, but days later, travelling again along the A38 in the early hours was astonished to see the same person standing at the same spot in the same weather conditions. Again he was picked up and, as requested, dropped at the bridge. That anyone should try to hitch a lift at such a time and in such conditions even once seemed unusual, but to do it twice seemed incredible: yet a month later he was there once more: the rain, the darkness, the mackintosh, the torch and the conversation were the same. Mr Unsworth felt that he was dealing with someone who was mentally disturbed, and was relieved when in the months that followed, although he frequently passed the spot at night, he saw no more of the stranger.

But in November 1958 he was there again, and like a bizarre film, the sequence of events went round once more—except that on this occasion when they stopped at the bridge the man asked if the lorry could wait while he collected some cases as he wished to go further along the road. For twenty minutes Mr Unsworth waited in the pouring darkness, and then, as the man had not reappeared, he drove on. Three miles ahead, however, he saw dimly through the murk of the streaming rain a torch being waved frantically to flag him down. Assuming it was a motorist who had broken down, he slowed up, but when his headlights shone fully on the figure, he saw with rising fear the long grey straggling hair and grey mackintosh of the mysterious passenger he had dropped earlier. No vehicle had passed in either direction, and it would have been quite impossible to cover the distance on foot in the time.

Now thoroughly alarmed, Mr Unsworth swerved to one side to pass the gesticulating figure, but as he did so, the man leaped in front of the lorry at such a distance that it was impossible to avoid a collision. But there was no impact: Mr Unsworth braked heavily, his articulated vehicle jack-knifed slightly, but on the deserted road remained under control and came to rest a few dozen yards ahead. He dismounted and looked back: the figure was still in the middle of the road, shaking his fist and swearing loudly at having been left behind. Then suddenly he was silent, turned his back, and with the final imprecation still tingling on the dripping air, vanished. With his hair rising, Mr Unsworth leapt

'A month later he was there again: the rain, the darkness, the mackintosh, the torch and the conversation were the same.'

The bridge at Holcombe where the hitch-hiker asked to be dropped off.

The man was seen standing in the middle of the road near the Heatherton Grange Hotel.

into his cab and drove furiously to where something like normality existed.

It is impossible even to guess at the identity of the apparition as so many motorists and pedestrians have died on this stretch alone. Perhaps one day, in a different manifestation, it may add another clue as to why this pathetic figure seems doomed to seek a lift so desperately from passing vehicles.

Collated from diverse sources

Seen But Not Known

Some psychologists believe that our dreams are not connected narratives, but a series of random people, places and objects. In its near-waking state the human mind, with its intense dislike of anything incomplete or irrational, joins these separate items into a logical story. Something similar may happen when people search for the antecedents of ghostly phenomena. This is well illustrated by the events at Pembroke in 1955.

Bush House, Pembroke, the family home for centuries of the Meyrick family, was demolished after a bad fire at the beginning of the century and rebuilt in 1905 as a grand mansion in the *fin de siècle* style. But fifty years later taste, the social climate and the cost of upkeep had changed so dramatically that after standing derelict for some time the house was sold to the local authority to be converted—in a last glorious fling of the tripartite educational system—into the boarding house for the new Pembroke Dock Grammar School which was being built nearby.

Among the workmen employed on the site were two Mancunians, George Hesketh and his son Roy, and a young Italian, known only as Toni. In August 1955 all three were asked to find alternative accommodation as their landlady had relatives coming to stay—a not uncommon situation for families who live near the sea. Unable to find other lodgings and refused permission by the clerk of the works to use the partly-completed school, the three men decided rather reluctantly to use, at least temporarily, one of the more habitable rooms on the first floor of the old Bush House. Not realising how brief their tenancy would be they built beds from waste timber and sacking and because the electricity had long since been cut off, acquired a Tilley (paraffin) lamp and made makeshift cooking arrangements.

They had expected the atmosphere of the empty, echoing and gloomy house to be a little disconcerting when everyone had left, but the first signs that something was more seriously amiss came late that night when the light from the lamp began to fade. When it was attended to it burnt up brightly, but almost immediately began to grow dim again. Simultaneously there came a continuous dull thudding on the doors and walls of the room. As the three lay in the darkness, tense, sleepless and silent, the Italian felt the overcoat he was using as a bed-cover being slowly but relentlessly tugged from him. Leaping up, he bolted the one door which still had a lock, and made sure the other would not open by nailing it firmly to the frame with battens of wood. But the hammering continued, and the following day, unable to face another night in the room, the men removed all of their belongings to a room on the top floor. Here, despite their apprehensions, all was quiet and uneventful, and exhausted by the previous twenty-four hours, they fell asleep quickly.

About 2am Toni woke, and felt drawn to the window that overlooked the garden wilderness below: a moment later his cries brought the Heskeths to his side, and they too saw, surrounded by an eerie light that made her clearly distinguishable, a lady 'dressed in a crinoline' walking steadily but soundlessly up and down a path beside the house. As the three men watched in terror—George Hesketh through binoculars he always carried—she moved towards an outhouse and seemed to melt through the ivy-covered wall. That was the end: grabbing their clothes they tore out of the building, and carefully avoiding the track where they had seen the apparition, they ran to the new school where they spent the rest of the night, uncomfortable and shivering. In the morning, fortified by the daylight and their mates, they examined the wall where they had seen the figure disappear, and found under the ivy traces of a bricked-up doorway. A few days after the Heskeths' experiences, a National Serviceman and his girlfriend ambling after dark through the grounds, fled when they saw a female form surrounded by a luminous glow approaching them.

But stranger still was the story of David James, an elderly man who had been night watchman on the site. On a light though moonless night some eighteen months earlier, he reported, he had been on his rounds at about 2am when he saw approaching a middle-aged man of medium height, dressed in breeches and leggings and carrying under his arm a double-barrelled shotgun. Three dogs trotted obediently at his heels. Puzzled because he knew that the man was not a local game-keeper and because it seemed unlikely that a poacher would behave in such a blatant manner, Mr James challenged him, first in English and then in Welsh. The figure, apparently neither seeing nor hearing, walked straight past, and when the night watchman turned to follow, stranger, dogs and gun vanished into a small pond.

The separate incidents were, of course, too exciting not to be woven into romantic tragedy: a Meyrick lady (at some indefinite date in the past) was returning home in her carriage, and as her husband came forward to greet her, he stumbled and accidentally shot her. In remorse he committed suicide in the pond. This may be true, but I can find no record of such an incident. If the dress was indeed a crinoline, the dates should be narrowed to about 1855-1875, but popularly any long full skirt tends to be called a crinoline, and clothes of this kind would embrace almost any period from antiquity to the twentieth century.

Regrettably, the Bush House ghosts must at present join the crowded ranks of the unidentifiable, but they may well be Meyricks, even if from different ages, appearing, as is so often the case, when there is a physical change in the surroundings of their corporeal existence.

Collated from diverse sources

No Dogs

It is widely believed that dogs are particularly sensitive to psychic presences, and the fact that dozens of correspondents have mentioned that their pets have shown signs of extreme agitation some time before they themselves have had an experience of the supernatural adds substance to the theory. But no account of animal sensitivity is more dramatic than that which took place at Meonstoke in 1975–76.

Meonstoke House is one of those homes that houselovers dream about: the central block was built in 1713 as the rectory in an architectural style so elegant that one wonders why it was ever abandoned. A southern wing added in 1870 maintained the lines of the original structure, but an addition in the arrogant 1920s strikes a slightly discordant note. This vanishes however as one stands on the terrace overlooking the formal lawns and garden that fall gently away down the slopes of the Meon valley to the lake below. Inside the rooms have the grace and space and proportions of an age that moved more leisurely so that it had time to regard the home as a thing of beauty and not merely a convenience living unit.

In November 1975 when Alen and Valerie Warner moved in they brought with them their family pet, a 3-year-old English sheepdog named Wanda, which they had had since a puppy and whose behaviour was impeccable in every way. She had travelled widely with the family to their cottage in Somerset and to the homes of friends so that she was familiar with strange surroundings and treated them all with the phlegmatic calm characteristic of the breed. But the moment she crossed the threshold of Meonstoke House, she became as if berserk, dashing to and fro in great agitation. The Warners were surprised at her unprecedented and almost hysterical excitement, but assumed that it must be the unaccustomed situation that was upsetting her, and that in a few days at most she would be her normal self.

But Wanda's behaviour steadily deteriorated: during the day she cried constantly as she scratched at the door to be let out, and once outside she howled dismally to be let back in. Immediately inside, she began her restless padding up and down. At night things were even worse: all through the hours of darkness she prowled about the house, rejecting her familiar bed and blankets, and refusing to lie down. By the morning she was exhausted. When she was confined to the hall—a huge room more than 40 feet long—she became almost demented. Although she was perfectly house-trained, she became filthy in her habits, and after three months of desperate efforts to find an answer, the Warners, sadly and reluctantly, were forced to ask their vet, if he could find her a good home. Some days later, in a completely strange farmhouse with a family she had never met before, Wanda reverted to her previous perfect behaviour.

An odd sequel occurred a few weeks later when Alen was in the village pub. One old man on learning that he was the new owner of Meonstoke House asked if he had a dog, and how it behaved. When told of Wanda's extraordinary activities the old man said, 'I've known that house for well over fifty years, and no one has ever been able to keep a dog there—they all go wild . . .'

With Wanda gone, the whole affair seemed settled—and then the front door bell began mysteriously to ring on its own. On the first occasion, early in 1976, Valerie and her 15-year-old daughter Joanna were alone in the house when there was an imperious and urgent peal on the bell. Joanna answered it, but there was no one in the large porch outside: assuming that some village boys were playing a joke, she closed the door and stood immediately inside ready to swing it open the moment the bell was touched again. A few minutes later the desperate clangour began again as if someone had a message of immense importance, and while the sounds were still on the air Joanna hurled open the door. Outside there was nothing but the blackness of the night and the moaning of the wind in the trees.

Three more times in the next twelve months came the peremptory summons, twice when Valerie was alone in the house, and once when she was with her 16-year-old son. In the latest incident, in February 1977, the bell rang five times during the evening, but every time the door was opened the sounds ceased. It may be coincidence, but on each occasion the bell has sounded like this the front door has been locked as well as fastened, as if whatever was outside resented that a corporeal body could not enter.

One other peculiarity of Meonstoke House is the small door on the first floor landing from the original building to the nineteenth-century wing which refuses to stay closed at night no matter how carefully it is fastened. The carpentering seems perfect, and of its own accord the door does not swing in either direction. During the daytime, too, it stays firmly closed or open.

Meonstoke House seems to have had a relatively uneventful history, as indeed it should as the home for most of its life of prosperous country parsons—though even in ecclesiastic circles, particularly in the eighteenth century, no one was ever quite sure what went on behind the austere but beautiful facade of house and profession. Perhaps the only time the building really stepped outside its regular and orderly role was in the early years of the twentieth century when there was a derailment on the single track Meon Valley Railway line which ran a few hundred yards behind the rectory. As Meonstoke House was the nearest shelter the casualties were brought across the fields and placed, one assumes in the great front hall.

Mr and Mrs Alen Warner, Southampton

The Chuckling Phantom

The remarkable events that occurred to two ladies in July 1947 when they were holidaying in Cornwall have ever since been the source of intrigued speculation and bewilderment to them. Miss Frances Robinson and her friend, Miss Roberta Probert, both in their forties, decided to celebrate the end of the war by renting a caravan for a fortnight in the well-known Cornish holiday village of Perranporth. When they arrived there late in the afternoon, however, they were disappointed and annoyed to find that instead of a new mobile home they had been allocated something that was little more than a dilapidated wooden shack consisting of a tiny living room, a bedroom and a kitchenette. As it was fairly early in the season and consequently many of the other chalets and caravans were unoccupied, they felt that they had been rather shabbily treated, but tired after the journey, and conditioned by eight years of strict austerity to accept whatever scraps of pleasure came their way, they settled in. After washing, a meal and unpacking, they went to bed early to read.

About 11pm they were greatly alarmed by the sound of stealthy footsteps padding round the outside of the building, and of a dog growling at the front of the house. Both women peered through the bedroom window, but as the night was very dark and overcast, they saw nothing. Hoping that the walls, flimsy though they were, would provide a sufficiently strong moral, if not physical, barrier to a potential intruder, they settled back uneasily to their books.

Suddenly there was the sound of the front door, which understandably they had locked and bolted with scrupulous care, being opened and then slammed shut. As the reverberations died away, they were aware of the same padding steps prowling round the living room. Horrified, Miss Probert called out, 'Who the devil is there?' A heavy silence followed, and both women prayed that the stranger had taken fright and had left, and was not waiting motionless but poised in the darkness a few yards away.

Then to their utter amazement they heard the rustling of paper as if someone was turning over the page of a large newspaper, and a gentle, jolly chuckle which was completely devoid of any malice or evil. It was as if a lunatic had entered and was enjoying a leisurely few minutes with an amusing article in the daily paper. The crinkling of the paper came again, followed by the laughter, and then an unidentifiable creaking noise. With considerable courage in view of their relatively lonely situation, the two women slipped from bed and advanced to the living room.

When they threw open the door the whole of the little room was visible in an instant: there was no one there, and nowhere anyone could hide. But with a tingling of their scalps they noted immediately that the wicker rocking chair was swaying to and fro with uncanny regularity. It was not the dying oscillations of a spring set in motion and left to run down, but the steady and equal rhythm of a chair being worked back and forth by someone invisible seated in it. Again from the chair came the eerie, but cheery, laugh, and the crackling of the paper, then as Miss Probert advanced, the low warning growl of an unseen animal which appeared to be located by the side of the rocker. Once more came the tiny titter, and a more insistent snarl from the phantom dog.

The women's nerves broke at this point. They fled back to the bedroom, locked the door and sat huddled under the electric light until dawn with senses taut and strained. From time to time they heard the footsteps padding round the house, and occasionally the happy laugh, but that was all. As the sun rose, they packed their cases and sat on the sand dunes until the rest of the camp began to stir. Another holiday maker gave them breakfast, and then they walked to the house of the owner. To their surprise she showed none when they told her their story, but said, 'I have heard similar stories from others.' She did, however, offer them one of her latest luxury caravans for the remainder of the holiday, and here the days and nights passed quite uneventfully.

It is impossible even to speculate on who this happy ghost may have been: perhaps an earlier, legitimate occupant of the cabin; perhaps the owner of an earlier building on the site, or even, at the limits of credibility, a vagrant who had surreptitiously settled in when the holiday visitors had gone, and who was amused at his own duplicity.

Miss F Robinson, Brighton